T0146984

Where is the Home of the Black Man?

Where is the Home of the Black Man?

EMMANUEL EHIOSUN

 iUniverse®

WHERE IS THE HOME OF THE BLACK MAN?

iUniverse books may be ordered through booksellers or by contacting:

iUniverse
1663 Liberty Drive
Bloomington, IN 47403
www.iuniverse.com
1-800-Authors (1-800-288-4677)

ISBN: 978-1-5320-7536-0 (sc)
ISBN: 978-1-5320-7535-3 (e)

Print information available on the last page.

iUniverse rev. date: 05/09/2019

CONTENTS

Dedication vii

Acknowledgement ix

Introduction xi

Chapter 1   The State of Africa in a Changing World ... 1

Chapter 2   Rich Resources, Poor Continent 19

Chapter 3   Rulers and the Politics of Slavery 31

Chapter 4   A Historical Look at the Human Race 48

Chapter 5   How to Move Africa Forward 61

Chapter 6   A Country and its People 77

Chapter 7   Modern Day Slavery- A Choice 93

Chapter 8   The Road to Exile 102

Chapter 9   Could Religion Be The Answer! 113

Chapter 10   Arise Africa, the Future is here! 124

Conclusion 131

Reference 135

DEDICATION

I hereby dedicate this book to the entire black race across the globe, and to encourage and remind you of our heritage. We're a people of great treasures and value.

God has blessed our land; our heritage and by no means must we fail to be what God intend for us all. Let's embrace the white race and not intimidate them in any way or remind them of their past. It is time to move forward and create a better tomorrow for our generation, so that as we grow older and weak, we will have peace here on earth.

It is time to take Africa back in our focus to revive our motherland, the land of our great ancestors.

ACKNOWLEDGEMENT

I want to acknowledge God Almighty, the creator of the heavens and earth. The one and only who paid the price for my freedom, Jesus Christ. All praise and thanks to him.

To my wonderful family and household, my parents, Mr and Mrs Ehiosun for the upbringing and values you invested in me, to my siblings, the awesome experiences we had growing up as children in our home. I want to thank you all for your support and prayers.

I want to honour my pastors over the years for the encouragement and prayers Dr.Sharp Okoro, and Dr.Wilberforce. Bezudde, Pastor Fortune Imariagbe, Pastor Dan.Tawari, Brother katte Nkorni, and Pastor Edward (cam).

To those whom I have admired and inspired by, Bishop T.D Jakes, Oprah Winfrey, Steve Harvey, Dr.Sunday Adelaja, Pr.Barack Obama. You've done a great job in the community of black race and created a mirror for us to see how beautiful we are and given us the courage and hope that we can make it. Thank you for being you.

To my wonderful Editor, Mr Clement Ogedegbe, thank you for the great job and your consistency in perfection and timely delivery. You're a great guy.

Mrs.Disu Adeola, wow, you are the best graphic designer on earth. I was marvelled to see you bring to reality the idea I had in mind concerning the book. Thank you so much for your effort, may God richly bless you.

INTRODUCTION

This book is based on cross generational historical background of the African race and western colonial experience over the years of slavery and national/ international independence of the African continent and the African diaspora in the western world. The cultural and intercultural values and systems of leadership which creates the bridge of understanding over the years of slavery, as the mentality of the people grew in one direction of race issues. Has it occurred to both races that it's not a race issue but a fight for superiority and a low esteem factors for what both worlds have common and uncommon, keeping the balances and an awareness of the usefulness of our natural resources for humanity.

Where did it all begin? Why did it happen...? Who are the victims? Who are the successors of the victims? Was it a choice of the victims? What have we done about it over the years? Will there be a future for Africa? And afterwards what will the westerners do if that happens. Will they feel vulnerable or guilty; or rather feel redeemed as it doesn't just end in granting independence. (Africa's independence hasn't been a solution yet). See through the contents of this book as you read with an eye of a deeper understanding to recruit a different mentality of the new age, cutting through and into the future of a better world for our children's children. The world should advance with a better living and mental understanding just as technology and science has been a more focused agenda. We must understand that without a renewed mind-set, even our technology and science have no meaningful value for humanity, it only becomes an abuse and will cause more damage. Human race must have knowledge and understanding first, before any other agenda for prosperity.

CHAPTER ONE

The State of Africa in a Changing World

Of all the continents of the world, none has been as unprogressive and undeveloped as Africa, the home of the black man. Although history has it that humans originated from Africa and that the continent is the second largest and second most-populous continent in the world, present realities show that Africa is the poorest and least civilized continent in the world.

The present day Africa is plagued by extreme hunger, poverty, wars and ethnic crisis, political unrest, illiteracy, terrorism, lack of infrastructure, lack of steady power supply, lack of portable drinking water, and a lot more plagues that are too numerous to mention.

Sub-Saharan Africa is the region with the highest infant mortality. On average, one in eleven children dies before his fifth birthday. Three of the four countries with the highest infant mortality worldwide are on the African continent: Ethiopia, Nigeria and Kenya.[1]

Africa is currently in a lamentable state. While the rest of the world is quickly changing and advancing, Africa has refused to take a step in the forward direction. While the rest of the world moves towards their future developmental goals and breakthroughs in medicine and technology, Africa seems to be moving in the opposite direction; regressing and going backward.

How a continent could be so big and yet have little or no development is the question that comes to the mind of many! How could it be that the continent that is said to be the oldest in the world lacks the expertise to advance itself and compete with the rest of the world! Could something be wrong with the black race!

There are many reasons one could say are responsible for the pitiable state of Africa today. I will however discuss three of them in this chapter. They are the poor mindset of the people, a lack of foresight and the inability to think creatively.

The Mindset That Limits Us

"Nothing can stop the person with the right mental attitude from achieving his goals. Nothing on earth can help the person with the wrong mental attitude." — Thomas Jefferson

Nothing else limits a person as much as mindset does. The mindset of a people determines how close to or far away they would be from progress, how civilized they would be and whether they would be able to advance their nation or leave it in a stagnant or regressive state.

For, Africa, we have been limited by no more than our mindset. Most Africans think that the major limitation to the development of our continent is the influence of the white man, the lack of resources or the slave trade. However, I do have a different view. It is my belief that our major limitation is not the influence of the white man; neither is it that we lack resources or are suffering from the effect of the slave trade, but that we have a faulty mindset. Our mindset is our major limitation. Until we change our mindset, we would not be able to change Africa.

I have heard many Africans say that the black man is cursed and that because of the curse, Africa will never be able to advance and progress. They say that nothing good can come out of Africa no matter how hard she tries. You only need to talk to an African about the future of Africa to find out how hopeless and doubtful most Africans are about the possibility of Africa ever becoming the leading continent in the world. Only a handful of Africans still believe that Africa could ever become a great continent, only a few believe that Africa could ever be as developed and civilized as the rest of the world. The remaining; the greater percentage of the African populace, have a mentality that is dominated by thoughts of inferiority, low self-esteem, and worthlessness. They see their skin color as a curse and a disadvantage. They see themselves as slaves to the white man and helpless without his intervention. Little wonder, even our African leaders look forward to aid from America and Europe before they could do anything of worth in their nations. It is not a surprise that we look forward to the white man to solve our problems for us. I am not surprised that our people are migrating en masse to Europe and America. It is all a function of our mindset. That mindset of limitation and inferiority has done much more harm to us than slave trade and colonialism could be blamed for.

Our mentality must change completely if we would build an African continent that the world would admire.

"No great improvements in the lot of mankind are possible until a great change takes place in the fundamental constitution of their modes of thought." — John Stuart Mi

If we as Africans do not change our thought pattern and wrong mental attitude, we would never be able to advance our continent. All Africans both home and abroad must learn that there is nothing wrong with the black man. We must come to the realization that we are not slaves to the white man or inferior to him. Our people must come to terms with the fact that everything we need to develop Africa has already been given to us by God. We have the resources, the land mass, the huge population and the intellectual capacity to rule the world. We have the history, the archeological facts that humans first existed in Africa and if we would look at the earliest civilizations of the world, we would be able to draw strength and hope from the fact that Africa once brought civilization to Europe and the world at large. This at least would go a long way to convince us that we are not a cursed race.

We are a gifted race, a highly intellectual people and an abundantly blessed continent. Our forefathers with this same black skin empowered the global society in science, in technology, in agriculture and in medicine, just to mention but a few. They influenced their world and future generations after them with their contributions and intellectual prowess. They are a proof that nothing is wrong with the black man. They are a proof that the black man is capable of anything and of everything if he sets his mind to do it.

Among them are the likes of George Washington Carver, Elijah McCoy, Dr. Patricia Bath, Marie Vann Brittan Brown and a host of others.

George Washington Carver was an African-American who discovered over 300 different uses for peanuts, including cooking oil, printer's ink, and axle grease.

He was born a slave in Missouri in 1864, at the time of the Civil War. As a child, George had an interest in plants and liked to collect specimens.[2]

Being a curious child with initiative and determination, George left home at age 11 to pursue an education. In 1894, Carver earned his bachelor's degree in agricultural science from Iowa State, and then his master's in 1896. At that time, he demonstrated a rare talent for identifying and treating plant diseases. Carver used agricultural chemistry and scientific methodology to improve the lives of impoverished farmers in southeastern Alabama.

Due to his crop rotation model of agriculture, Carver harvested a lot of sweet potatoes and peanuts. However, not many people ate them. They were not crops with many uses or applications. They were undesirable crops.

Resourceful and inventive as he was, Carver started to work on inventing new food, industrial and commercial products such as flour, sugar, vinegar, cosmetic products, ink, paint, and many others came out from these sweet potatoes and peanuts.

Dr. Carver developed hundreds of new products from peanuts and created a new market for these inexpensive, soil-enriching legumes. He repeatedly said that he was always happily working to make the world a better place to live. He believed his inventions could contribute to this purpose.

George Washington Carver died in Tuskegee, Alabama, on January 5, 1943. He is acknowledged and remembered as one of the most sensitive and creative scientists of all times and all races.

Elijah McCoy was another black man that greatly influenced the world with his inventions. He was born in 1844 in Ontario, Canada. He was the son of fugitive slaves who escaped slavery from Kentucky through the Underground Railroad, which was a code name, and a system used to escape slavery from 1820 to 1861.

Safe and free in Ontario and despite having very little resources and being extremely poor, Elijah's parents worked hard to save money for their son's education.

At the age of 15, Elijah's parents sent him to a boarding school in Edinburgh, Scotland where he learned mechanical engineering through an apprenticeship. Back in the United States as a certified mechanical engineer, McCoy found it difficult to obtain a job as a skilled African-American. Instead, he accepted a job as a fireman for the Michigan Central Railroad oiling the various working parts of the trains. McCoy had plenty of time to think while performing this very slow and boring task. It was then when he developed his curiosity in the challenges of self-lubrication for machines. The moving parts of the trains had to be lubricated by hand, and he began to develop and test his ideas for automatic lubrication.

McCoy finally developed the Lubricator Cup in a device that continuously dropped small amounts of oil onto the moving parts of the machines. In 1870, his Elijah McCoy Manufacturing Company began to produce his lubricators. He received the patent number 139,407 for his Lubricator Cup on May 27, 1873. The lubricator cup allowed steam trains to run continuously without pausing for maintenance, saving time and money to owners who insisted on buying McCoy lubrication systems. Soon it became common to hear that machinery buyers would take nothing less than The Real McCoy.

For over 25 years, McCoy kept on refining his invention and receiving a patent for every update and modification of the lubricator cup. He received over 60 patents over the course of his life.

Dear friend, can you see how these black men born in the days of slavery impacted the world and contributed greatly to the wellbeing of many generations after him! How could George Carver have invented over three hundred products if the black race was cursed or if anything was wrong with being black?

How could Elijah McCoy have received over 60 patents for his invention if the black man has nothing to offer to the world!

Truly, there is nothing wrong with the black man; we only need to change our mindset. We are not a hopeless people; we only need a new mindset. We are not a handicapped race; we only need to develop a new mentality. All through history, the black man has proven himself intellectually sound and capable of anything as long as a human can do it.

We however, do not know our history and are void of the knowledge that all through the ages black men and women have changed the world positively. The average African knows little or nothing about how Africans have contributed greatly to the progress of the world, how world civilization began in Africa, and how Africa is greatly endowed with mineral resources. Our history is not being taught in schools and if perhaps, it is taught; only a vague idea of it is transferred to us. We know little or nothing about how great Africa was before the white man came to our shores but know almost everything about the fact that the white man colonized us. The unbalanced and one-sided knowledge that we have about our history as Africans has created so much inferiority complex and a feeling of self-insufficiency among our people. We are left with no self-worth and are kept in a state where we continually look at the white man as our Lords and masters.

"The worst thing that colonialism did was to cloud our view of our past."

— Barack Obama

However, it is enough! We must change our mindset; we must teach our people that we have all it takes to build a continent; one that can lead all other continents of the world. We must bring orientation to all Africans that we can saturate the world with the greatest inventions in medicine and technology. We urgently need to renew our minds if Africa will lead the world again. It is not about slavery or colonialism. It is about our mindset!

Without Foresight, Nation Building is Impossible

The word foresight is one word, but I have separated the word fore-sight for a proper survey to look at what it really means. The word FORE means before, prepare, prior to, to perceive, and to plan. The word SIGHT means to see far, to visualize something, which you want to do ahead or to see the future in an imaginary state of mind, to strategize its execution and to bring it to life.

People often perceive things with their eyes, which I call vision but vision can also be described as what someone thinks will happen or occur in the future, whereas FORE SIGHT is planning for things before they happen. Everything that makes the world around us was brought to life through the ability of proper planning and research. All the great nations of the world that we see today and that we love to migrate to, did not become great by magic or miracle but through careful planning and research. Without foresight, no nation can be built into a great nation. In the same vein, no continent could become a leading continent in the world without proper planning and execution.

America was carefully planned and executed. Europe was consciously planned and built. The same goes for every other continent of the world. Unfortunately, for our motherland Africa, it is unplanned.

Looking into the years past and now in the present, Africa has failed to plan her future. It is not that we lack the ability to see our future and plan for it, but have rather refused to do so. We live with the mentality of instant gratification and prefer only to consume everything today than plan for the future. We think only in the short term, and when it's all exhausted, we go back to start all over again to continue the same routine process of eating everything now and now and never planning for tomorrow. We seem not to realize that without planning no nation can be built. We completely ignore the words of Benjamin Franklin when he said:

"If you fail to plan, you are planning to fail!"

— Benjamin Franklin

The reason Africa is failing is not that the black man does not have the capacity for progress but that she (Africa) has failed to plan her future. If we actually do well in our planning, we will not be stock with same systems of government and let corruption creep in to disorganize our future. The question then is" why don't we plan the future of our continent?" The answer is mind-set! It all boils down to our mind-set. How can we plan our future as a continent, when we believe that nothing good can come out of Africa! How can we draw a plan to build our nations when we have a preconceived idea that we will forever be subject to the white man's ideas and that we can never do anything without the help of the white man! How can we consciously draw a plan for the development of Africa when we have made up our minds to run to Europe and America to seek a safe-haven!

That being said, I want to challenge you if you are an African reading this book that we all can sit down and plan Africa. I want to challenge you to get rid of any preconceived idea that limits us from building our own land. Let us get the past behind us, and look at the great future that lie ahead of us. We can make Africa a leading continent in the world if we believe we can and join hands to plan the development of our nations.

Instead of looking at the past, I put myself ahead twenty years and try to look at what I need to do now in order to get there then. – Diana Ross

Independence without Creativity

Many years ago, our ancestors from various African countries fought tooth and nail to break free from the rule of the white man. From Nigeria, to Zimbabwe, from Kenya to democratic republic of Congo, from Ghana to Gambia, and across many other African countries, men and women gave their time, energy and risked their lives to fight for the liberation of the African continent from colonial rule.

For what were they exactly fighting? They wanted a continent in which a black man would rule each individual country with black racial heritage and not one in which each country would be subjected to the dictatorship of the white man. They were fighting for self-rule. They were seeking independence and self-governance. They wanted to build their individual nations by themselves and manage their God-given resources as they chose to and not as the colonial masters dictated for them.

That was a good fight! It was a noble and a courageous thing to do. What was the outcome of the fight? Independence! Yes independence. Almost all African countries that fought so hard for independence eventually got it. Our fathers got what they wanted. They broke free from colonial rule and each black nation became an independent nation.

Nigeria got her independence in the year 1960. Ghana got theirs in 1957, Gambia in 1965, Kenya in 1963, Congo DR in 1960 and Zimbabwe in 1980. This is just to mention but a few.

In a speech by Kwame Nkrumah, the first prime minister and president of Ghana, while he moved the motion for the independence of Ghana before the House of Commons[3], London in 1953; he urged the House of Commons to give the Ghanaian government the freedom to rule her people by herself and to bring their dreams of independence to reality. He said that the black people of Africa and Ghanaians in particular had dreamt for many years to be freed from the rule and Lordship of the colonial masters who had seized and stolen their African heritage and right to self-governance from them. Kwame Nkrumah argued that it was time for Africans to be given back their God-given rights to live as free people who should not be dominated over by the white colonialists. He said boldly to the House of Commons that he and his fellow countrymen had resolved to claim back their right to independence. And that this right to independence is not an exclusive preserve of the white skinned humans but that of all humans. It was in that meeting that Kwame Nkrumah boldly declared to the white colonialists that it was wrong for any nation either because of its military strength, economic capability or intellectual capacity to deprive or deny other less privileged nations their right to independence. In rounding off his speech, he convinced the House of Commons that Africans were prepared and ready to assume responsibility for self-rule and that he was sure that if granted independence, Africa would build a continent that the rest of the world would be proud of.

It was with high hopes and an unshakeable faith in the future of Africa that our fathers fought for independence as one could see from the speech given by Kwame Nkrumah above.

Unfortunately, many decades after we got independence from the colonial masters, nothing much can be said of Africa's progress and development. It is almost as if we are worse off now than we were under colonial rule.

Looking at the present realities in Africa today, one is tempted to conclude that Africa has made little or no progress since independence until now. What could be the problem! Why have we not been able to build and develop our continent, as we should? The answer is not far-fetched. We lack the creativity to build a nation and more so a continent. To say that we lack the creativity to build a nation may not describe the exact nature of the black man but only the condition in which he finds himself thanks to ignorance. Every human, whether black or white is created in the image and likeness of God and hence, has the nature of God: the creative nature of God inclusive.

Before God created the habitable earth that we see today, record has it that the earth was without form and void. Then God began to create everything that man would need to make the earth habitable and enjoyable. The creative nature of God was displayed at creation and it began with foresight. God saw everything that man would need and through proper planning, created them into existence. Creativity begins with foresight, and foresight begins with preparation for action. Before God created the human race, he first made available the environment and resources for man to survive. Afterwards he then made man in his image and likeness, giving man the power and dominion over everything he created, and most importantly urging man to further the creation process. This he did by charging man with the command "be fruitful, multiply and replenish the earth".

According to this principle, every human being is supposed to be a creator. It does not matter the skin color, we all are supposed to make the earth a better place by creating everything else that we know would make life easy and accessible to all human being. That is the reason we would have maximized our creative ability to create the kind of continent that the world would admire after we gained our independence as a continent. We would have projected towards the advancement of a continent that future generations to come would see and be proud about.

Unfortunately, instead of us to create the Africa of our dreams, we were simply carried away with the joy of independence that we forgot to plan, envision and create a continent that every black man would be proud to call home. Today, decades after Africa's independence, the black man can hardly call Africa his home. He looks for the slightest opportunity to run away from his motherland to go stay in the white man's country. One is therefore forced to ask, "Where is the home of the black man"

It is for this reason, that I have written this book: to answer the question of "home for all black men and women, the question of identity, and the question of Africa's future development and emancipation."

I want to challenge my fellow Africans to begin to think creatively and not just live complacently in the Euphoria of independence from colonialism. The creative ability that the white man has so demonstrated to build the beautiful continents of Europe, America, and Australia etc. lies within each and every one of us as black men and women. We must use our foresight, plan and create an Africa that we can call home.

It is my belief that having independence from colonial rule means nothing, if we Africans fail to creatively advance our continent. It is true that we are a free people. Now that we are free, the question before us is "What is next for Africa, what does the future hold for us?

We can only meet the challenge of our age as a free people. Hence, our demand for our freedom, for only free men can shape the destinies of their future.

-Kwame Nkrumah

Nuggets 1

1. Africa is currently in a lamentable state. While the rest of the world is quickly changing and advancing, Africa has refused to take a step in the forward direction.

2. While the rest of the world moves towards their future developmental goals and breakthroughs in medicine and technology, Africa seems to be moving in the opposite direction; regressing and going backward.

3. Nothing else limits a person as much as mindset does. The mindset of a people determines how close to or far away they would be from progress, how civilized they would be and whether they would be able to advance their nation or leave it in a stagnant or regressive state.

4. It is my belief that our major limitation in Africa is not the influence of the white man; neither is it that we lack resources or are suffering from the effect of the slave trade, but that we have a faulty mindset.

5. Our mindset is our major limitation. Until we change our mindset, we would not be able to change Africa.

6. The mindset of limitation and inferiority has done much more harm to us as Africans than slave trade and colonialism could be blamed for.

7. Truly, there is nothing wrong with the black man; we only need to change our mindset. We are not a hopeless people; we only need a new mindset.

We are not a handicapped race; we only need to develop a new mentality.

8.   All through history, the black man has proven himself intellectually sound and capable of anything as long as a human can do it.

9.   The unbalanced and one-sided knowledge that we have about our history as Africans has created so much inferiority complex and a feeling of self-insufficiency among our people. We are left with no self-worth and are kept in a state where we continually look at the white man as our Lords and masters.

10. Without foresight, no nation can be built into a great nation. In the same vein, no continent could become a leading continent in the world without proper planning and execution.

11. The reason Africa is failing is not that the black man does not have the capacity for progress but that she (Africa) has failed to plan her future.

CHAPTER TWO

Rich Resources, Poor Continent

In the previous chapter, we discussed the state of Africa in a changing world. In this chapter, we shall discuss why Africa is the wealthiest continent in the world and the poorest at the same time.

The Wealth of Nations

It is no longer news that the countries of Africa are among the poorest countries in the world. I believe that this is a fact that every honest black man both home and abroad agrees with.

There are several reasons that have been given to try to explain why Africa, the oldest continent in the world is also the poorest. Chief among such reasons is the idea that the white man is to blame for Africa's impoverished state. Those who accuse the white man for the beggarly condition of Africa after over 50years of independence from colonial rule are simply living in the past and have refused to live in the present or look towards the future. It is either they have forgotten that the white men left our shores about 5 decades ago or they are aware but just choose to play the blame game.

It is a pity that this is the disposition of most of our African sons and daughters. They have taken it upon themselves to continually blame the white man for the present economic setback and poverty that has become synonymous with Africa all over the world today. It is indeed a heartbreaking reality to know that whenever the name Africa is mentioned on the world stage, the thought that comes to mind is poverty, underdevelopment, and extreme hunger.

Having said that, the question I would like us to answer in this book is this "is Africa really poor, does she deserve to be poor?"

The answer to that question is "No!" Africa is not actually poor.

Africa is blessed with a rich bounty of natural resources. The continent holds around 30% of the world's known mineral reserves. These include cobalt, uranium, diamonds and gold, as well as significant oil and gas reserves.

Researchers have even found out that the amount of mineral resources deposited in just one African country by the name of Democratic republic of Congo is worth $24 trillion and that this amount is more than the total

GDP of the United States, Germany, China, Japan and the United Kingdom summed together. That is just one country out of about 54 countries that make up Africa. How is it then that Africa could be said to be poor, if one out of 54 countries has mineral resources worth more than the combined GDP of the top five economically stable nations of the world.

Important reserves of natural resources, like petroleum and precious metals, are the bulwarks for laying the foundations for the future.

-Enrique Pena Nieto

Africa is indeed not poor. We have all the resources for which a continent could be called rich. We have everything that could make any nation of the world a great nation. We have the mineral resources, the land mass, the population, the intellectual capacity, the universal gift of time.

What then do we lack that qualifies us to be called a poor race, or an impoverished nation? Nothing substantial: Except the fact that we have failed to build a prosperous continent with everything that we have at our disposal. We have failed to advance our continent with the natural blessings (resources) that we have been so graciously given by God. We have simply failed to take advantage of our huge mineral resources and large population to build an enviable continent. We are taking for granted the privilege of being so highly endowed with the natural resources that are hugely lacking in countries like Japan, Singapore and South Korea.

Having very little natural resources (most of the mineral deposits in Korean peninsula is ironically located in North Korea); South Korea has managed to rise to become the 15th largest economy in the world. The South Korean economy is still expanding and it is one of the best performers among developed nations. Nevertheless, South Korea, in the most famous example given by World Bank, went from an African standard nation (in par with Ghana) in the 1960s to one of the world's leading industrial powerhouse today.

The same is the case for the mountainous, volcanic island country, Japan. She has inadequate natural resources to support her growing economy and large population, hence dependent on imported raw materials.[1] However, Japan is now the world's third largest economy.

It is a shocking reality for most people to find that with no natural resources and having a very small population, Singapore shows the world how a tiny island can likewise become one of the world's most prosperous and advanced economy. Having virtually nothing in its island, they have been able to build a nation that every black man wants to run to and call home.

From the foregoing, we could see that if nations that are lacking in mineral resources are regarded as rich nations today, Africa with all its abundant resources should and deserve to be called a wealthier continent. We are an abundantly rich race.

However, despite being so richly endowed, and despite the mining boom of the past decade, Africa has drawn little benefit from this mineral wealth and remains one of the poorest continents on the globe, with almost fifty per cent of the population living on less than $1.25 per day.[2]

So, why is it that a continent with such vast potential wealth can remain so poor practically? The answer is ignorance!

Ignorance-Our Greatest Enemy

Our only poverty is that of knowledge. We lack the knowledge to transform our wealthy mineral resources into practical riches and into prosperity for our citizens. If we are a practically poor continent, it is not because we are void of the natural resources needed to build a prosperous Africa that we can call home, but because we are ignorant of how to convert our wealth into tangible and enviable riches. Our greatest enemy therefore, is not the white man but our ignorance. Our greatest limitation is not racism, colonialism or lack of mineral resources. Our greatest limitation is our ignorance.

"Ignorance is the greatest slave master in the universe."

— Matshona Dhliwayo

The reason the black man with all the mineral resources in his soil goes to Japan, South Korea, and Singapore; countries with little or no mineral resources, to go find greener pastures and settle there, is not a lack of resources, a lack of independence, but ignorance. If we must build a continent that we can call home, we must enlighten our people. We must make the acquisition of knowledge a priority. We must eradicate ignorance from our land. It is true that we have independence and self-rule now, but until we kill ignorance in Africa, we would not be able to create a continent that would become the envy of the world.

"Knowledge will forever govern ignorance, and a people who mean to be their own governors, must arm themselves with the power knowledge gives. A popular government without popular information or the means of acquiring it, is but a prologue to a farce or a tragedy or perhaps both"

— *James Madison*

There has to be a new era for Africa, an era of knowledge, an era of understanding. There has to be a new beginning, a new day for the man of color, a day in which the quest for knowledge will become the priority of all and sundry. That day is now. The time is ripe. We must get knowledge and understanding. We must get the wisdom that is needed to convert our huge mineral resources into national and continental prosperity for our people. It is time to through wisdom and understanding build an Africa for which the entire black race will be proud.

The reason the world is changing and Africa is behind is that we have not given priority to wisdom and understanding. Until we teach our people that knowledge, understanding, and wisdom are what are needed to build a continent and not just independence, we would hardly be able to build the Africa of our dream.

In stressing the importance of wisdom, knowledge and understanding as it regards building a house, a nation, a continent or anything at all, the writer of proverbs wrote:

Through wisdom a house is built,

And by understanding it is established;

By knowledge the rooms are filled

With all precious and pleasant riches

Proverbs 24:3-4 NKJV

From the verses above, we see that a house, nation, continent etc. is only built through wisdom and without understanding, its chambers cannot be established. In addition, we see that all precious and pleasant riches can only be brought to a nation, continent or home by knowledge.

That is to say, if Africa must alleviate itself from poverty, it must study, research and imbibe the knowledge that is needed to convert all the huge mineral resources in its soil into tangible riches and economic prosperity for all its citizens. Our continent is perishing for lack of knowledge. Until we get knowledge, we will continually regress and remain in the dark. Until we get knowledge, the white man, despite our independence will still rule over us.

Everything the world may need to advance itself settles in Africa. If we must advance our continent, every citizen of Africa must make the acquisition of knowledge a priority.

There is no more room for self-pity and the blame game. We no longer need to wait for foreign nations to come to our aid. We only need to learn how to build a prosperous nation and an economically stable continent. We need to educate ourselves.

"Education is for freedom - freedom from mental slavery."

— *Ogwo David Emenike*

With knowledge, we would live truly free. Without it, we would remain mental slaves.

True Freedom versus Mental Slavery

"Mental Slavery remains the biggest form of oppression till this day. New insights or idea is what shines freedom from such an oppression."

— *Unarine Ramaru*

I once read a story of a dog owner who constantly chained his dog to an iron pole allowing the dog to walk only a limited distance everyday while in chains. Whenever the dog attempted to walk past that distance and go further, the chains with which it is tied to the pole restricts it. This it did for many years until the dog got used to that limited distance and concluded that it will never be able to walk a longer distance. One day the owner of the dog unfastened its chains and the dog was no longer bound and restricted. Surprisingly, the dog walked only to that limited distance that it was accustomed to and stopped. It could not even attempt to go further. What had happened? The dog is unaware that it could go further. Although the physical chain that limited it from going further had been loosened, yet the dog was still bound in its mind. It could not go further than the limitation it had in its mind.

This story reminds me of Africa and the black race. We were many years under the ruler-ship of our colonial masters; we were treated as slaves, restricted from expressing our thoughts, maximizing our potentials and building our continent. Thankfully, our fathers fought for independence and we became a free people. However, though we are free, a lot of us are still bound in our minds. We are still under a kind of slavery that I call mental slavery. We are not any different from the dog in the story I shared above.

We have everything it takes to build and advance our continent, yet we would not and the reason is that we are still enslaved in our minds. We do not think or believe that we have everything it takes to build an enviable continent. We do not believe in our potentials. We do not believe that we have the capacity to grow and progress just like Europe and America. Hence, we would rather run abroad than build our nations. We have made up our mind to return to our slave masters to serve them; this time around not because they held us bound in chains but because we have become mental slaves. The average black man does not want to build his own continent; he wants to migrate to the white man's own. What a pity!

"These negroes aren't asking for no nation. They wanna crawl back on the plantation."

— Malcolm X

So, why is Africa poor? Is it because we lack mineral resources? No! We have an overflowing abundance of it.

Are we poor and underdeveloped because the white man denied us freedom of self-rule? No! They granted us independence about 60years ago.

I would like to state here that one major reason Africa is a poor continent despite its vast mineral resources is the slave mentality that has plagued the lot of its people. Although we are free from colonialism and slavery, we however, are still mentally captive and until we renew our minds, we would not be able to build Africa and become a developed continent.

As I begin to round off this chapter, I would like to state that Africa is indeed a blessed continent. We are a wealthy people and have everything we need to build a leading continent.

The onus is on us to educate ourselves, kick out ignorance from our continent and then renew our minds from mental slavery. Once we do this, we would be able to think creatively, see clearly, and use the power of foresight to plan and execute the creation of an African continent that we can all call home. In addition, Africa will no longer be termed a poor continent.

In the next chapter, we shall discuss how the rulers of Africa have brought underdevelopment and backwardness upon their own people.

Nuggets 2

1. Africa is indeed not poor. We have all the resources for which a continent could be called rich. We have everything that could make any nation of the world a great nation.

2. We Africans have failed to build a prosperous continent with everything that we have at our disposal. We have failed to advance our continent with the natural blessings (resources) that we have been so graciously given by God.

3. If nations that are lacking in mineral resources are regarded as rich nations today, Africa with all its abundant resources should and deserve to be called a wealthier continent. We are an abundantly rich race.

4. If we are a practically poor continent, it is not because we are void of the natural resources needed to build a prosperous Africa that we can call home, but because we are ignorant of how to convert our wealth into tangible and enviable riches.

5. Our greatest enemy is not the white man but our ignorance. Our greatest limitation is not racism, colonialism or lack of mineral resources. Our greatest limitation is our ignorance.

6. The reason the black man with all the mineral resources in his soil goes to Japan, South Korea, and Singapore; countries with little or no mineral resources, to go find greener pastures and settle there, is not a lack of resources, a lack of independence, but ignorance.

7. If we must build a continent that we can call home, we must enlighten our people. We must make the acquisition of knowledge a priority. We must eradicate ignorance from our land.

8. It is true that we have independence and self-rule now, but until we kill ignorance in Africa, we would not be able to create a continent that would become the envy of the world.

9. Until we teach our people that knowledge, understanding, and wisdom are what are needed to build a continent and not just independence, we would hardly be able to build the Africa of our dream.

10. We have everything it takes to build and advance our continent, yet we would not and the reason is that we are still enslaved in our minds.

11. Although we are free from colonialism and slavery, we however, are still mentally captive and until we renew our minds, we would not be able to build Africa and become a developed continent.

CHAPTER THREE

Rulers and the Politics of Slavery

I have written in the previous chapters of this book about the abundant wealth of Africa, her freedom from colonial rule and sadly, her backward and deplorable state. In this chapter, I want us to look at the root cause of our problems and the possible solutions to them.

Enslaved By Our Own Rulers

Africa's economic malaise and stunted developmental growth is not the result of lack of resources, the influence of colonialism or the supposed inherent inability of the black man to achieve anything of worth. It is rather due to the inability of our leaders to manage the continent, as they should.

While they fought for independence, the founding leaders of Africa's independence had one goal in mind, to be given the liberty to lead Africa to the Promised Land without the interference of the white man. Under colonialism, our fathers dreamt that independence would come with the opportunity for the black man to prove to the world that he is capable of running his own affairs.

The vision they had for Africa was grandiose, and it reflected in the speech given by Kwame Nkrumah at the House of Commons in London, 1953. I deem it fit to paste an excerpt from it here again. It says:

If there is to be a criterion of a people's preparedness for self-government, then I say it is their readiness to assume the responsibilities of ruling themselves. For who but a people themselves can say when they are prepared. How can others judge when that moment has arrived in the destiny of a subject people?"

-Kwame Nkrumah

Despite the belief by our founding fathers that we Africans were prepared and have what it takes to rule ourselves, the stunted growth of Africa and the pitiable state she finds herself today seems to be a far cry from what one would have expected.

Right from the days of independence, Africa has had numerous political rulers cut across its member nations. What have they all done to Africa? How well have they ruled the nations of Africa? Well, the answers to the questions are glaring. What is before us today is a continent of poverty, lack of infrastructure, hunger, illiteracy, ethnic wars, corruption, political unrest, to mention but a few.

Has our leadership failed us? Of course, yes! Africa's problem is no more than a leadership problem. While many argue that leadership is not the problem of Africa, we cannot however deny the fact that *everything rises and falls on leadership* as John C. Maxwell once said.

From the foregoing, we can say that if Africa is in ruins, the leadership is to blame. If Africa is in prosperity, the leadership is to praise. Everything rises and falls on leadership.

The deplorable state of Africa today, many years after fighting for self-rule leaves the western world and Africans alike with doubt about the possibility of Africans being able to manage the affairs of their own countries.[1]

Much of what the majority of our past and present African leaders have been able to do is to blame the white man for the failure of Africa to progress and to, continually depend on the western world for aid before making any major leadership decision.

The result of such dependency is a new type of slavery. The whole of Africa is enslaved again; however, this time by its own rulers.

There are two ways African leaders enslave their own people; firstly by bringing the entire country they have been elected to govern under the leadership of the formal colonial masters from whom we claim to have gotten independence. When African leaders cannot make their own decisions but rather live only by the dictates of the western world, one cannot but call that slavery. If we need the USA and the UK to tell us how to run our countries, then we are still under colonial rule and are not independent nations. So it is that our leaders enslave us by bringing us under the rule of the colonialists.

The second way that African leaders enslave their own people is via oppression, political tyranny, cruelty and corruption.

Africa is as underdeveloped and backward as it is, not because of the oppression from the white man, but because of its rulers and political tyrants. In Africa today, we are enslaved by our own rulers, and oppressed by the political tyrants.

Although, most Africans still accuse the white man of taking us to their land as slaves, it is however a fact that we willingly travel there by ourselves today, doing everything possible and risking our lives to go there. Ironically, our former colonial masters, actually still welcome us to their countries, keep us in a healthy condition and provide the necessary amenities that our own African nations have failed to provide for us.

The white man is no longer our oppressor; our own African leaders are our new oppressors. The land of the white man is way more conducive and homey for many Africans today than our own embattled countries. Our African leaders steal government money and buy landed properties in foreign countries for themselves and their immediate families. They deprive their own people of quality education, good medical care, good roads, potable water supply, electricity and power supply, and almost all the basic amenities that the citizens of any nation would need to survive. Most African leaders intentionally impoverish their own citizens and leave them in a beggarly state where they are forced to lament and beg for the resources that are rightfully theirs to be able to survive. The common wealth of each African nation is shared among only a few political cabals and godfathers, while the rest of the populace is left to die in hunger and economic recession. The political class lives in million dollar houses, have their own private jets, go for holidays in exorbitant locations; and this they do using stolen public funds, while the common man is left to thrive with less than two dollars a day.

It might interest you to note that Africa just recently recorded the highest rate of modern-day enslavement in the world. Armed conflict, state-sponsored forced labor, and forced marriages were the main causes behind the estimated 9.2 million Africans who live in servitude without the choice to do so, according to the 2018 Global Slavery Index.

In recent years, serfdom in the continent has attracted global attention after videos showed "slave markets" in Libya where African migrants were being auctioned off in car parks, garages, and as well as public squares.[2] The question is "Who was selling the African migrants?" Other black African men!

Do not be surprised, the white man is not our problem. We are our own problems. We have always enslaved ourselves. Our rulers have always enslaved our own people even before we got independence.

For centuries along the West African coast, millions of Africans were sold into slavery and shipped across the Atlantic to the Americas.

The middlemen were European slave traders based in forts like Ghana's Cape Coast Castle, now a tourist attraction and a sombre reminder of a brutal crime against humanity.

That crime is usually blamed entirely on the European outsiders who inflicted slavery on African victims. But new research by some researcher supports a different view - - that Africans should share the blame for slavery. Why should they?

"It was the Africans themselves who were enslaving their fellow Africans, sending them to the coast to be shipped outside," says a certain African researcher.[3]

From the foregoing, it is obvious that Africans themselves are to blame for not only the pre-independence slavery but also the modern day slavery of the black race by its political rulers. Could it be that our political leaders freed us from the colonial masters only to become our slave masters! Perhaps yes!

"Many if not most slaves would have each readily jumped, and many if not most slaves would each

readily jump, at the opportunity to be a master, if such an opportunity presents or had presented itself." —Mokokoma Mokhonoana

We cannot pretend to be blind to the enslavement of the black race by its own political leaders. One way in which such oppression and enslavement is displayed is via political disenfranchisement. Across Sub-Saharan Africa, many groups are excluded from political participation because of their ethnicity, religion, gender or region. They often face violence, threats, neglect, and exploitation. The political oppression of these groups is systematic and primarily state-driven.[4]

Until we Africans begin to fight for the total freedom of the black race, we will not be able to build a continent that we can proudly call home. The question however, is "who will fight for the freedom of the black African man?

Who Will Fight For Africa?

There is need for freedom fighters to arise and fight for the liberty of all sons and daughters of Africa, from the slavery and oppression that is being meted out to all by our own political class and rulers. We cannot all seat down and watch a few people truncate the destiny of our continent just because they have political power. We cannot just fold our arms and let our fellow brothers enslave the rest of us just because they were privilege to procure political power. We must all rise up and fight. Freedom as we know does not come easily as though it is freely given to the oppressed. No! It is demanded and fought for. If our fore-fathers never fought for independence we would not have it today. We would still be under colonial rule today, had courageous and well-meaning Africans not fought for the liberation of the African continent.

As a student of history, I have come to realize that all through history, whenever a people are oppressed and enslaved, God usually raises other people to fight for them and win their freedom.

The nation of South Africa once had what was regarded as apartheid, which was a system of institutionalized racial segregation that existed from 1948 till early 1990's. It was a form of political rule in which the white people of South Africa oppressed the black majority, deprived them of their basic human rights and treated them as second class citizens.

It was at such a time that Nelson Mandela, a man who could not stand by and fold his arms seeing how his fellow black men were humiliated and dehumanized rose up to the occasion and took it upon himself to fight for the freedom of the black man. His dream was to see a South African nation in which there were equal rights for all irrespective of skin color. He envisioned a nation in which no one would be enslaved because of his or her skin color.

To bring about freedom for his fellow Africans, he joined a political party; led peaceful protests against the apartheid government that oppressed the black people of South Africa and did all he could to fight for the freedom of the black man. His actions eventually led him in prison and made him spend about three decades of his life behind bars. Thankfully, he was released from prison and became the first black president of South Africa and the man who completely eradicated slavery and oppression in South Africa.

In declaring his willingness to fight against oppression and slavery at any cost, he said:

"During my lifetime I have dedicated myself to this struggle of the African people. I have fought against white domination, and I have fought against black domination. I have cherished the ideal of a democratic and free society in which all persons live together in harmony and with equal opportunities. It is an ideal which I hope to live for and to achieve. But if needs be, it is an ideal for which I am prepared to die."

-Nelson Mandela

It is true that Nelson Mandela fought for the liberation of the black man and envisioned a nation in which all citizens would have equal rights.

However, it is a sad reality today that the average African political leader finds pleasure in enslaving his fellow African people. In almost every African country today, it is oppression and enslavement. I wonder whether African leaders have any moral grounds to condemn South Africa. Which African country is a democracy in the true sense of the word?" This in no way justifies apartheid, but it calls attention to the flagrant injustices heaped upon black Africans by their own leaders - the very same leaders who self-righteously lead the march to free the blacks in South Africa. Even Bishop Desmond Tutu, a Nobel laureate and staunchly anti-apartheid, can see through this transparent hypocrisy.

In a recent remark, he lamented: ***"It is sad that South Africa is noted for its vicious violation of human rights. But it is also very sad to note that in many black African countries today, there is less freedom than there was during that much-maligned colonial period."***

Dear friends, we must all say no to any form of slavery against the black race irrespective of who the oppressor is. The white men left our land many years ago and many decades later, slavery still resides in our land. Our people are enslaved by a few political tyrants of same color and origin. We must do everything we can to fight against it. We must resist all forms of oppression in our continent. Do not ask who will fight for Africa? You and I are the ones to fight for Africa. Nelson Mandela is dead, but we are here. We must fight for the freedom of our people. It does not matter who the slave masters are; black or white, we must resist them.

Until the world recognizes that oppression is oppression, irrespective of the skin color of the tyrant, it has no business pontificating about ``freedom" for black Africans.[5]

Paul Biya: 86years old Cameroonian President for the past 37years!

Teodoro Obiang Nguema Mbasogo: 76years old President of Equatorial Guinea for 40years!

José Eduardo dos Santos: 74years old President of Angola for 38years!(from 1979 to 2017)

Yoweri Museveni: 74years old President of Uganda for 33years!

Omar al-Bashir: 75years old President of Sudan for 30years!

Idriss Déby: 66years old President of Chad for 29years!

Isaias Afwerki: 73years old President of Eritrea since independence in 1993!

The above listed, are a select few from a longer list of African leaders who are yet to consider anyone else fit for their 'democratic' thrones, despite spending an incredible number of years in power.[6]

All these leaders have ruled Africa for so long and yet no visible progress can be seen in the economic growth or developmental growth of Africa. Our brothers and sisters still prefer to migrate abroad and feel safer there than remain in our backward continent. Our political tyrants have not been able to build a home for the black man. And unless, we all rise up to resist these slave masters, we will not be able to build a home for the black man in Africa.

Nuggets 3

1. Africa's economic malaise and stunted developmental growth is not the result of lack of resources, the influence of colonialism or the supposed inherent inability of the black man to achieve anything of worth. It is rather due to the inability of our leaders to manage the continent, as they should.
2. If Africa is in ruins, the leadership is to blame. If Africa is in prosperity, the leadership is to praise. Everything rises and falls on leadership.
3. When African leaders cannot make their own decisions but rather live only by the dictates of the western world, one cannot but call that slavery.
4. Most African leaders intentionally impoverish their own citizens and leave them in a beggarly state where they are forced to lament and beg for the resources that are rightfully theirs to be able to survive.
5. God is always interested in sending a lifesaver, a deliverer or a savior to rescue an enslaved people.
6. Africans can never be set free from political slavery until the people themselves are willing to be set free. As long as the people love their oppressors, they would remain in oppression. Not

even God would be able to help a people who are not willing to be helped.

7. One of the reasons Africa is as backward and underdeveloped as it is today, is that the black man keeps fighting against his deliverer and loving his oppressors.

CHAPTER FOUR

A Historical Look at the Human Race

Having said so much about the lamentable state of the African continent, it is needful to explain at this point, how it all got started. How come the black race is so deprived and how did the slave trade begin? These and a few more questions will be addressed in this session.

Slave Trade & the Civilization of the Black Race

In the previous sessions, we stated that Africa is the oldest continent in the world and that the black race is the mother of the modern human. The question however that bothers most Africans is "how the oldest continent turned out to become the continent of slaves and colonized people"

History has it that Africa is the home of the world's most ancient civilizations. Africa was the cradle of the world and provides a comprehensive and contiguous time line of human development going back at least 7 million years. Africa, which developed the world's oldest human civilization, gave humanity the use of fire a million and half to two million years ago. It is the home of the first tools, astronomy, jewelry, fishing, mathematics, crops, art, use of pigments, cutting and other pointed instruments and animal domestication. In short Africa gave the world human civilization.[1]

And not only that, the African soil is richly endowed with minerals and natural resources. Africa has the richest concentration of natural resources such as oil, copper, diamonds, bauxite, lithium, gold, hardwood forests, and tropical fruits. It is estimated that 30% of the earth's mineral resources are found in the African continent. Additionally, Africa has the world's biggest precious metal reserves on earth.[2]

Africa's economic and social development before 1500 is assumed to have been ahead of Europe's. The economic growth of Europe in the 13th and 14th centuries was initiated and enhanced by Africa. That was possible thanks to the gold from the great empires of West Africa, Ghana, Mali and Songhai. The Europeans were drawn to Africa also because of the wealth of Gold that is buried in African soils.

In the 14th century, the West African empire of Mali was larger than Western Europe and was said to be one of the wealthiest and most powerful states in the world.

Once in 1324, the emperor of Mali, Mansa Musa visited Cairo, and took so much gold with him that the price of

Gold lost its value and became so cheap that even after 12years, its worth could hardly be restored.

Despite the wealth of natural resources, Africa is still underdeveloped and is still remembered in history as the depot for slave trade.

How did it happen? How did a continent so rich and so old become the poorest continent in the world? History tells us why.

In the mid-fifteenth century, Africa and Europe started a mutual trade that ruined and depopulated Africa, but on the other hand, enhanced the wealth and growth of Europe. It was from that time till the last part of the 19th century that Europeans began to buy African captives as slaves.

Initially, this human trafficking of Africans was only to supplement the human trafficking that was already ongoing within Europe. Yes Europeans were already enslaving each other before they turned to Africa. It is also important to note that slave trade was also already prevalent amongst Africans before the Europeans started buying Africans. Most Africans were sold off by their fellow Africans to Europe, the Middle East and other parts of the world before the slave trade of the mid-15th century.

The usual route through which most of these African captives got to Europe and other parts of the world was through the Sahara. The slaves usually exited North Africa, or travelled via the Indian Ocean.

Portugal was the first to travel overseas and reach Africa to buy slaves. Later on, other European empires followed suit and that was how the transatlantic slave trade began. The Portuguese began by kidnapping Africans from the west coast of Africa and taking them to Europe to be their slaves.

Portugal took so many slaves to the extent that by the early 16th century as much as one out of every ten persons in Lisbon was of African descent. Soon after the Europeans discovered America, there was increased need for more African slaves.

The Spanish were the first to take African slaves to America from Europe. That happened in 1503, and by fifteen years later, the first slaves have been transported directly from Africa to America.

Although historians have not completely agreed as to how many slaves were sold out of Africa within the next four hundred years, a report in the late 1990s gave an estimate of over 11 million people. Many of these slaves died on the way without reaching their destination.

Although the Europeans and the Americans often take the blame for the slave trade in Africa, I must say that the Arabs also need to share a part of the blame. The Arabs were also heavily involved in slave trading. The total number of Africans taken from the continent's east coast and enslaved in the Arab world is estimated to be somewhere between 9.4 million and 14 million. These figures are imprecise due to the absence of written records.

One historian estimated that, approximately 5 million African slaves were transported by Muslim slave traders via the Red Sea, Indian Ocean, and Sahara desert, to other parts of the world between 1500 and 1900.[3]

The forced removal of up to 25 million people from the continent obviously had a major effect on the growth of the population in Africa. It is now estimated that in the period from 1500 to 1900, the population of Africa remained stagnant or declined.

The human and other resources that were taken from Africa contributed to the capitalist development and wealth of Europe.

Africa was the only continent to be affected in this way, and this loss of population and potential population was a major factor leading to its economic underdevelopment.

The transatlantic trade also created the conditions for the subsequent colonial conquest of Africa by the European powers and the unequal relationship that still exists between Africa and the world's big powers today.

Africa was impoverished by its relationship with Europe while the human and other resources that were taken from Africa contributed to the capitalist development and wealth of Europe and other parts of the world.

Historians have long debated how and why African kingdoms and merchants entered into a trade that was so disadvantageous to Africa and its inhabitants.

On the African side, the slave trade was generally the business of rulers or wealthy and powerful merchants, concerned with their own selfish or narrow interests, rather than those of the continent.[4]

No Race Is Superior to Another

One of the results of the slave trade was a division of the human race: with one race, parading itself to be superior and the other blatantly believing that it is inferior. This unequal relationship between the human races is a consequence of the enslavement of Africans. The prevailing ideology of racism at the time was the notion that Africans were naturally inferior to Europeans.

In fact, the ideology that the white man is superior to the black man was one of the reasons why colonialism succeeded. Africans allowed themselves to be colonized because they believed they were inferior.

Today, many years after the era of the slave trade, most Africans still see themselves as inferior to the white man. The white man on the other hand lives with the supremacist ideology that was born out of the slave trade and the colonial dominance over Africa.

However, as I earlier stated, there is nothing wrong with being black just as there is nothing good with being white. We are all humans, whether black or white, it does not matter.

"We were all humans until race disconnected us, religion separated us, politics divided us and wealth classified us." ~anonymous

If we, as Africans are ever going to be able to build a continent that we can call home, we must all come to the understanding that no race is superior to another. Every one of us must see ourselves as equally endowed and gifted as the white man is. Cultivating this mindset is very crucial to the development of Africa because low self-esteem incapacitates and deprives one of the ability to maximize one's potentials. Low self-esteem destroys human potential and leads to inactivity. The man who sees himself as inferior and good for nothing, will never dare to explore the world to see what he can create and make for himself. He would perpetually depend on others whom he has come to believe are better than him. This is why, the black man whose mind has not been enlightened will never attempt discovering anything new or creating an invention. He waits to always consume or use what the white man has created. If you are wondering why little or no inventions spring out of Africa, you may want to consider low self-esteem as a factor. An entire continent full of people who see themselves as inferior and less –gifted will never be able to rule over and lead another whose citizens see themselves as superior and highly gifted. If Africa must become a leading continent in the world, we must first teach our sons and daughters that we are not inferior to the white man. We must believe in ourselves that we have whatever it takes to build an enviable continent, then go ahead, and build it.

Reconciliation Must Be Total

Having said that the black man is not inferior to the white man and vice versa, I would like to say here that for us to be able to walk with this mentality and build a new Africa, we must reconcile with the white man. It is true that they once treated us as inferior humans. It is true that the white man bought our fore fathers as slaves. No one can deny the fact that: the white man harshly treated our ancestors in the days of colonialism. However, I would like to say that, that is all gone now. It is all past. We must stop seeing the white man as our enemy. We must put the past behind us and reconcile with the Europeans and Americans. They left our lands many years ago. They gave us independence many decades ago and no longer impose their will upon us as a continent and as individual nations. Today, they accept us when we migrate to their country. In addition, they allow us to enjoy their high-class educational system. They give us the best medical care, the type that is lacking in our continent. They send aid every year to the impoverished nations in our continent. They give us loans when our leaders fail to manage our economy and squander our resources. The white man has been good to us if we are going to tell ourselves the truth. Millions of Africans are scattered all over Europe and America today enjoying the serenity, the infrastructure and every good thing that Africa has failed to provide for us.

To be sincere, Europe and America feels more like home to the majority of black people that migrate from Africa to settle abroad. Otherwise, our people would not have remained abroad and would have returned home in their numbers. Nevertheless, you will agree with me that the reverse is the case; more and more black sons and daughters of Africa are trooping to Europe and America every day to enjoy the white man's land.

It is on record that the European Union (EU) aid represents more than 50% of global aid. The EU and its member states provided €21 billion in development aid to Africa in 2016,

One third of the overall foreign direct investment in Africa comes from the EU with €32 billion invested in Africa by EU companies in 2015,

€3.35 billion is in allocation to the European investment fund for sustainable development, which should trigger up to €44 billion of investments.

The EU deploys several civilian and military missions across sub Saharan Africa.

€1.4 billion are committed to educational programs in Africa from 2014 to 2020.[5]

From the foregoing, it is obvious that the white man has been good to us. We must forgive the wrongs of the past and make peace with each other: both black and white. Colonialism is over. The slave trade is over. We must look forward to the future of Africa and prepare ourselves to build it the way we want it. In addition, for that to happen, reconciliation must be total.

"The truth is, unless you let go, unless you forgive yourself, unless you forgive the situation, unless you realize that the situation is over, you cannot move forward."

— *Steve Maraboli*

The Lack of Self-Identity

There is a huge number of black people all over the world today whom I believe can contribute to the development of Africa; the home of the black man. Of particular interest to me are the millions of black people living in America who are together, called by the name black Americans or Afro-Americans. Why am I interested in this group of people? It is because; I believe they have a great role to play in the development of Africa. Unfortunately, many of them do not want to have anything to do with Africa, be associated with the blacks in Africa or even accept the name *black Americans*. The reason for this is that these people have suffered an identity crisis over the years. Being born in America and having lived there all their lives it is easy to see why they would have such a crisis. Until someone tells them about their history, they would hardly even consider that they are Africans.

So, who is a black American or an African American?

According to encyclopedia Britannica, African Americans are one of the largest of the many ethnic groups in the United States. African Americans are mainly of African ancestry, but many have nonblack ancestors as well.

African Americans are largely the descendants of slaves—people who were brought from their African homelands by force to work in the New World.

Africans assisted the Spanish and the Portuguese during their early exploration of the Americas. In the 16ᵗʰ century, some black explorers settled in the Mississippi valley and in the areas that became South Carolina and New Mexico. The most celebrated black explorer of the Americas was Estéban, who traveled through the Southwest in the 1530s.

The uninterrupted history of blacks in the United States began in 1619, when 20 Africans landed in the English colony of Virginia. These individuals were not slaves but indentured servants—persons bound to an employer for a limited number of years—as were many of the settlers of European descent (whites). By the 1660s, large numbers of Africans were being, brought to the English colonies. In 1790, blacks numbered almost 760,000 and made up nearly one-fifth of the population of the United States.[6]

From the foregoing, we see that the black Americans are the descendants of black ancestors who got to America either to work or as slaves. These black ancestors, lived in America, married in America and gave birth to children in America. All through the years, the offspring of these black ancestors have contributed to the growth and development of America. Sadly, they have forgotten or know little or nothing about their origin and have done little or nothing to develop Africa, their motherland.

It is my wish that just as black Americans have contributed to the growth and development of America, so also should they now turn to Africa to develop and grow it.

One cannot detach one's self from one's origin no matter how hard one tries. We all as black people must be proud of our origin. We must be proud of our identity.

It does not matter whether you are in America, Europe or Africa, we must all join hands to build our continent. If Africa is to become developed, there is need for all black people all over the world to cultivate a positive self-identity. Furthermore, this positive self-identity must inspire us all to work together for the good of Africa and the world at large.

Nuggets 4

1. One of the results of the slave trade was a division of the human race: with one race, parading itself to be superior and the other blatantly believing that it is inferior.
2. Africans allowed themselves to be colonized because they believed they were inferior.
3. If we, as Africans are ever going to be able to build a continent that we can call home, we must all come to the understanding that no race is superior to another. Every one of us must see ourselves as equally endowed and gifted as the white man is.
4. Low self-esteem incapacitates and deprives one of the ability to maximize one's potentials. Low

self-esteem destroys human potential and leads to inactivity.

5. The man who sees himself as inferior and good for nothing, will never dare to explore the world to see what he can create and make for himself. He would perpetually depend on others whom he has come to believe are better than him.

6. An entire continent full of people who see themselves as inferior and less –gifted will never be able to rule over and lead another whose citizens see themselves as superior and highly gifted.

7. If Africa must become a leading continent in the world, we must first teach our sons and daughters that we are not inferior to the white man. We must believe in ourselves that we have whatever it takes to build an enviable continent, then go ahead, and build it.

8. Colonialism is over. The slave trade is over. We must look forward to the future of Africa and prepare ourselves to build it the way we want it.

9. If Africa is to become developed, there is need for all black people all over the world to cultivate a positive self-identity.

CHAPTER FIVE

How to Move Africa Forward

In the previous chapter, we discussed how the political class has constantly enslaved the citizens of Africa and brought stagnation to the growth and development of the continent. In this chapter, we shall discuss how to move Africa forward in the direction of economic growth and development.

Experience or Ideas!

Ideas they say rule the world. To move Africa forward, we must elevate ideas above political experience or better still have a combination of experience and ideas. To elevate experience above ideas or choose experience in place of ideas is to program a nation for failure. It does not matter how much political experience you have, if you are void of ideas, you will never be able to build a competitive nation or continent. That is the exact problem with Africa. We keep choosing leaders with political experience but zero ideas.

The result is 50 or 60years of independence with nothing to show for it except economic recession, lack of infrastructural development, ethnic and religious crisis, insecurity, corruption, terrorism and every other societal vice that you can think of.

We are the poorest continent in the world not because we have leaders who are politically inexperienced but leaders who are void of ideas. I showed you in the previous chapter political tyrants who stayed in power for 37years, 38years and 40years with little or nothing to show for it. The men who have impoverished Africa and enslaved her are men of many years of political experience who are void of ideas. The political rulers who embezzle the commonwealth of their nations and leave the citizens bankrupt are men of many years of political experience.

The lamentable state of Africa that we see today is a product of many years of leadership by experienced men. Experience has done us no good in Africa. If we keep allowing experienced men who are void of ideas to lead us, we will never be able to build an enviable continent or nation. Experience is good but if it is not mixed with ideas, it leads to destruction and disaster.

What do we have in our political sphere today?

We have men who are experienced in stealing public funds.

We have men who are experienced in bribery and corruption

We have men who are experienced in election rigging

We have men who are experienced in assassination and extrajudicial killings.

We have political leaders who are experienced in enslaving the citizens.

Africa is home to experienced political juggernauts that have zero idea about nation building.

The crop of old political rulers in Africa today, has made complaining and playing the blame game their only specialty. They have little or no ideas to build a glorious continent.

You don't make progress by standing on the sidelines, whimpering and complaining. You make progress by implementing ideas.

-Shirley Chisholm

Many Africans argue today that experience is the key factor in building, and developing a nation. I say no! Ideas are!

Our founding fathers who fought for our independence, had little or no political experience, yet the days of their rule were the best days in the history of most African countries. All thanks to ideas.

History had it that in Nigeria for example, one naira of our currency was equal to one pounds of Great Britain's currency. That was when men who were without political experience but full of ideas ruled Nigeria.

In terms of economic sufficiency, the first fourteen years after independence were the best years for Nigeria. Within those years, the strength of the Naira was almost equaled that of the Dollar. The Nigerian currency could compete with that of Great Britain and we were regarded as one of the fastest growing economies of the world.

The years from 1960 to 1973 were also the best years in terms education, standard of living, and employment.

Other areas like health and per capital income were also far better than what we have today. Then there was free education, scholarship opportunities and automatic employments for fresh graduates. Those years were the years of ideas. It was less experience and much of ideas. And ideas built a nation that was glorious. Those who saw Nigeria in her former glory will weep when they compare those good old days to the shambles that is left of her today. It was not experience that gave us the glory then, it was ideas.

In those glorious years, the government was committed to planning and executing developmental goals for the nation. For instance, one of such plans, the second national development plan was set to experience 6.6% annual growth rate but surprisingly, it achieved an 8.2% GDP growth rate. It was in those years that many roads were constructed, the 2nd Niger Bridge was built, the Federal Scholarship Scheme was established, and refineries were established. The Ajaokuta Steel Mill and the national youth service corps (NYSC) scheme were all established within those years. The country was also able to use the proceeds from exports of cocoa, rubber, cotton, groundnut and palm produce to establish universities like the University of Nigeria Nsuka, Ahmadu Bello University, Zaria and Obafemi Awolowo University, Ife.

Cities that are not as endowed as Lagos also witnessed remarkable developments and became commercial centers.[1]

Today, we have experienced old men seating in the seat of power and upon huge wealth of natural resources and yet have no idea of how to build an economy. Today, African leaders seat on gold, diamond and oil but have no idea what to do with these resources.

Donald Trump was alleged to have said concerning Africa:

"You're not humans, how can you sit on Gold, diamond and oil and still be poor"

-Donald Trump

If we are honest with ourselves, we would agree with the assertion above. We are a poor continent today not because we lack resources, but because we have experienced leaders with little or no ideas.

Today, Nigeria is no longer a major exporter of cocoa, ground nut, palm oil, rubber and cotton.

The iron and steel industry is dead and the manufacturing sector is ailing. There is over reliance on oil. Over the years, our development planning efforts have been stalled by endemic corruption in the system. Today, there are no accurate data to plan the economy.

What am I trying to say? I am trying to say that a nation without ideas is a dead nation. A nation whose leaders are void of ideas cannot become a great nation. And more so, a nation whose leaders are void of ideas can hardly raise citizens with ideas. Imagine a nation or a continent in which both leaders and the masses are void of ideas; the result will be economic catastrophe, underdevelopment and retarded growth.

It is the duty of every leader to create ideas and build an environment that encourages citizens to create their own ideas also.

The role of a creative leader is not to have all the ideas; it's to create a culture where everyone can have ideas and feel that they're valued.

-Ken Robinson

Great nations are built thanks to ideas. And if Nigeria and Africa must move forward in development and economic growth, we must elevate ideas above experience or better still have a blend of the two. Ideas rule the world and if

Africa must become a leading continent in the world, we must pay attention to ideas, ideas and ideas!

Visionary Leadership is The Key

Although we have said so much about the slave trade and the colonization of Africa, I would like to say here that I do not think that those are Africa's greatest problems. The abolition of the slave trade happened long ago; the colonization of Africa gave way to independence many years ago. You and I cannot do anything about them anymore. Our greatest challenge now is that of leadership. Africa's greatest problem is leadership failure: the lack of visionary leaders.

To develop any nation or continent, the people who are in charge of leadership must be people of vision. Without vision, nation building is impossible.

"Good leaders have vision and inspire others to help them turn vision into reality. Great leaders have vision, share vision, and inspire others to create their own."

— Roy Bennett

According to Cambridge dictionary, the definition of the word vision is *"The ability to imagine how a country, society, industry, etc. could develop in the future and to plan for this:"*

From the definition above, we see that vision has to do with the imagination of how a country or society could develop. It is seeing into the future and planning to achieve it.

Unfortunately, African leaders are mostly visionless leaders. They lack the ability to see into the future of their countries, plan towards that future and then execute those plans. I am of course not surprised why that is so. As we stated earlier, the majority of African political rulers are old men who have refused to relinquish power to younger generational leaders. It is not in the nature of old men to be visionaries. Even the holy scriptures attest to that. The Jewish prophet Joel while prophesying said:

And it shall come to pass afterward, that I will pour out my spirit upon all flesh; and your sons and your daughters shall prophesy, your old men shall dream dreams, your young men shall see visions

(Joel 2:28 KJV)

From the above prophesy, we could see that God's promise to humanity does not include old men seeing visions. Old men can only dream. Vision is a thing for the young men.

I therefore, do not expect a Robert Mugabe of Zimbabwe at the age of 94 to have been able to build a first world nation. Old men are visionless! It is not in their nature to have visions.

I do not think that 85 years old Paul Biya of Cameroon has anything good to offer the country as it relates to economic growth and national development. Old men lack the capacity to have visions! They only dream.

If you are expecting an Alpha Conde at the age of 80 to be able to build a first world Guinea Bissau, you are not being truthful to yourself. Old men do not know how to envision and plan the future. They live in the unrealistic world of dreams.

I believe that a president Mohammad Buhari of Nigeria at the age of 75 does not have the blueprint to build a competitive economy. He could only do what old men do: sleep and dream.

President Teodoro Obiang Nguema Mbasogo of Equatorial Guinea is not any different. He is 76 years old and as expected, void of vision for a first world country.

I could go on and on mentioning these old men and why they can never build a first world nation. However, I would not do that for want of space.

The average age of the 15 oldest African leaders is 77; compared to 52 for the world's ten most-developed economies.[2]

Could this be one of the major reasons for Africa's under-development?

Yes! It takes visionary leaders to build countries and birth economic growth and development. Only young men can do that. Vision is not a thing for the old but for the young.

If Africa must become a continent of first world nations, the old crop of rulers that have mismanaged the continent and hindered its growth, must give way to young and visionary leaders to take the stage, who with their innovative ideas and intellectually sound minds would build an Africa that can compete with any other continent in the world. Otherwise, if we leave our continent in the hands of old men, they will keep dreaming and never achieve anything.

Embrace Change or Remain in Status Quo

One of the most difficult things for people to do, especially Africans is to accept change. Africans are too used to status quo that it is almost useless to try to introduce anything new to an African man. It does not matter if the status quo is a limitation to economic growth and development; the typical African would rather have a retarded economy and an underdeveloped country than think of accepting a change. It matters little to the African mind even if the status quo breeds corruption; he is ready to do anything to avoid change. It is not a surprise that Africa is the poorest and least developed continent in the world. It has a connection to our love for status quo and phobia for change.

The whole world is changing but Africa is still in love with status quo. The world has gone digital, Africa prefers analogue still. Our educational system is outdated. Our mode of power supply is obsolete. Our health care system is obsolete. Even our mode of conducting political elections is old fashioned. Wondering why our citizens prefer to vote for old men during elections, it is simple: love for status quo and dislike for change. The just concluded Nigerian presidential election attests to the point I am making. It did not matter to the citizens that the two old political parties (APC and PDP) comprise corrupt politicians who in the past have destroyed the country and squandered her resources: they still preferred to vote for them instead of the new political parties with young visionary leaders. You want to know why. Love for status quo and hatred for change.

How do you build a 21st century nation with such love for status quo and hatred for change! It is impossible. Until we are ready for change, we will never grow as a nation and as a continent.

The world is growing but Africa remains the same

-Bill Gates

If we are going to grow into an economically stable nation, we must let go of status quo and embrace change. If we are going to become a developed continent, our love for positive change must exceed our love for status quo. Without a love for change, civilization will only be a dream in Africa, it will never happen.

Every great nation you see today at some point in their history had to let go of status quo to embrace change. They did away with some culture. They let go some traditions. They amended some laws, all in an effort to build their economy and develop their nations.

Africa needs transformational leaders; leaders who would bring drastic change to the nations of Africa. Such leaders would undo hindering traditions, defeat superstitious and cultural practices that preclude civilization and encourage new and transformational ideas that support national development.

Such a leader in history was the man Saint Patrick. Ireland was a highly superstitious and uncivilized nation. The people loved their traditional practices and resisted any possible change. Their love for status quo was so strong that they would be willing to kill to protect it.

However, everything changed when a transformational leader in the person of St. Patrick came to Ireland.

Patrick of Ireland was an outstanding example of a man who disciple a nation. He was a world figure; one of the very great among men; —one of the dominant personalities of world history. He completely transformed Ireland in his lifetime and set the nation on its destiny.

In addition to multitudes of converts, Patrick worked to bring transformation in all spheres of life:

He saw untold thousands converted. He founded 700 churches. He trained and set in place Church leadership — 700 bishops and 3000 ministers. He set up training centers to educate thousands.

He transformed civil government, working with kings to establish godly laws.

"He worked so many miracles and wonders, that the human mind is incapable of remembering or recording the amount of good which he did upon the earth. He carried on his nation-changing work with great confidence in the Lord, but with great humility, writing in his Confessions

His work in Ireland was a world event. Historian Seumas MacManus writes:

All histories of all countries probably could not disclose to the most conscientious searcher another instance of such radical change in a whole nation's character being wrought within the lifespan of one man.

There was a complete transformation of Ireland from the time before and after Patrick. The people before Patrick were worshiping idols and —were carrying the ruthless law of the sword far over sea and land enslaving those they encountered. After Patrick, the worship of the living God was predominant throughout the nation, and the Irish people —left the conquering sword to be eaten by rust, while they went far and wide again over sea and land, bearing now to the nations— both neighboring and far off— the healing balm of Christ's gentle words[3]

It is such leaders as Saint Patrick that Africa needs. Leaders who would bring complete transformational change to the continent. However, more than just having a transformational leader, every citizen of Africa must be ready to embrace change and divorce traditions, cultures, and superstitious beliefs that hinder the growth and development of our continent. It is not enough to complain about the lamentable state of Africa. We must all be ready for change.

If you do not like something, change it. If you cannot change it, change your attitude.

– Maya Angelou

It is my belief that as we all embrace positive change just as the sons of Ireland did, we would be able to build an African continent that every black man can call home.

Nuggets 5

1. To move Africa forward, we must elevate ideas above political experience or better still have a combination of experience and ideas. To elevate experience above ideas or choose experience in place of ideas is to program a nation for failure.
2. It does not matter how much political experience you have, if you are void of ideas, you will never be able to build a competitive nation or continent. That is the exact problem with Africa. We keep

choosing leaders with political experience but zero ideas.

3. We are the poorest continent in the world not because we have leaders who are politically inexperienced but leaders who are void of ideas.

4. The men who have impoverished Africa and enslaved her are men of many years of political experience who are void of ideas. The political rulers who embezzle the commonwealth of their nations and leave the citizens bankrupt are men of many years of political experience.

5. If we keep allowing experienced men who are void of ideas to lead us, we will never be able to build an enviable continent or nation. Experience is good but if it is not mixed with ideas, it leads to destruction and disaster.

6. Today, we have experienced old men seating in the seat of power and upon huge wealth of natural resources and yet have no idea how to build an economy.

7. We are a poor continent today not because we lack resources, but because we have experienced leaders with little or no ideas.

8. To develop any nation or continent, the people who are in charge of leadership must be people of vision. Without vision, nation building is impossible.

9. It takes visionary leaders to build countries and birth economic growth and development. Only young men can do that. Vision is not a thing for the old but for the young.

10. If Africa must become a continent of first world nations, the old crop of rulers that have mismanaged the continent and hindered its growth, must give way to young and visionary leaders to take the stage, who with their innovative ideas and intellectually sound minds would build an Africa that can compete with any other continent in the world.

11. If we are going to become a developed continent, our love for positive change must exceed our love for status quo. Without a love for change, civilization will only be a dream in Africa, it will never happen.

CHAPTER SIX

A Country and its People

In the previous chapter, we explained how we could move Africa forward by combining ideas with experience, by electing visionary leaders and by embracing change. In this chapter, we shall discuss the role each citizen has to play alongside the government in other to turn Africa into a safe haven for every black person on the earth.

The Right Principles of Government

The nations of the world, called first world nations or developed nations did not get developed via magic. It was not through a miracle that nations like the United States of America, Singapore, Norway, Switzerland etc. became first world nations. All these nations became first world nations thanks to the careful and thoughtful application of the right principles of government.

We as black people are always in a hurry to migrate to developed nations but are sluggish when it comes to researching the principles with which the white men built these nations. Our leaders are quick to travel to Europe, America Australia and Asia for holidays, tourism and medical care but they do not stop to ask questions as to how those continents got to the enviable heights that we are still wishing to reach today. How do I know our leaders do not ask questions when they travel abroad? It is evident in their behaviors when they return. They return from their trip and do not do anything new in terms of national development. They return to continue the status quo.

They see state of the art hospitals, libraries, stadiums, roads, railways, universities, housing, technology etc. when they travel abroad and yet all they do is snap photographs and live in the euphoria of their experience when they return. They do not research the principles of government that are functional in those nations to replicate same back home. They return only to keep complaining and blaming the government they succeeded. It is almost as though they are ignorant of the fact that nations are great thanks to the right principles of government and not as a result of blaming and pointing fingers at previous leadership.

Governance plays a key role in the development and prosperity of a country. With good governance, it is possible for a small, resource-limited and young country to develop effectively and enjoy prosperity. Without good governance however, even countries endowed with abundant natural resources will not succeed.[1]

It is not enough to seek self-governance or independence; one must be ready to learn the right principles of governance as well. Otherwise, the result would be an impoverished and economically stunted nation.

Every African nation can become a first world nation by simply employing the right principle of government. All we need are leaders who are able to learn the right principles of government and citizens who are willing to live by them. Yes! It is possible to turn poverty-stricken third world African countries into first world countries. The only thing we need is the right principles of government. Lee Kuan Yew and his people did it in Singapore; we can replicate it in Africa.

Singapore is an example of how a third world nation can become a first world nation via the right principles of government.

Once known as a backward fishing village, Singapore now has one of the highest per capita GDP (about US$56,000) in the world. It is among the first ten most competitive economies in the world. The city-state is one of the best-governed countries, thanks to low crime rates and virtually no public sector corruption.

However, at the time of Singapore's independence, first from the United Kingdom in 1963 and then from Malaysia in 1965, virtually no one believed that a resource scarce Singapore could even survive. Its founding father Lee Kuan Yew, once remarked that 'an independent Singapore was a political, economic and geographic absurdity.'

How Singapore has transformed itself from a third world country to a first rated nation? A host of factors is responsible for its rapid development. Chief among them are the application of the right principles of government. Lee Kuan Yew's astute leadership guided the country on its way to greatness. Samuel Huntington termed him one of the 'master builders' of the 20th century. Mr. Lee and his successors ensured that a small but very efficient government runs Singapore.[2]

What are the principles of governance with which Lee Kuan Yew was able to turn third world Singapore into a first world country?

Principle 1: Meritocracy

The number one priority of the government of Singapore is education. Every child in Singapore is entitled to a formal education. The goal of the government is to have no single illiterate in Singapore. This offers every Singaporean a chance to advance up the social ladder, where everyone is judged by his or her capabilities, and not by race, religion or background.

Principle 2: Racial and religious harmony

In Singapore, racial and religious harmony is viewed as more important than the freedom of speech and freedom of press. The Maintenance of Religious Harmony Act prohibits all forms of attacks on any religion. This is critical to building a multi-ethnic society in Singapore, where various forms of religions exist.

Principle 3: A clean government

Singapore adopts a zero-tolerance policy towards the elimination of corruption within its government and civil service. Ministers and senior civil servants have been jailed for such offences in the past.

Principle 4: Rule of law

According to a World Bank study, the rule of law ranks top among the factors influencing a country's development. With a sound justice system in place, everybody in Singapore is treated fair and equal. This gives confidence to businesspersons and investors, who know their money is placed in a protected environment.

Principle 5: Inclusiveness

Singapore views social equity as crucial in its growth strategy. The government subsidizes education, housing, healthcare and public transportation for all its citizens, even though it refuses to be branded as a welfare state. The heart of Singapore's social-economic system is made from a unique blend of capitalism and socialism practices.

Principle 6: Care for the environment

Since he came to power, former Prime Minister Lee Kuan Yew championed to clean up the river and streets of Singapore. He believed that a clean environment is critical to the development of the country. He turns down investments that could pollute the environment.

So what can you and I learn from these principles of government that would be needed to build an enviable Africa that we can call home?

It is simple:

The first principle is this: We need to give priority to education in Africa. One of the reasons for Africa's backwardness and stunted growth is illiteracy. The number of out-of-school children is alarming.

At least half of youth between the ages of 15 and 17 in sub-Saharan Africa are not in school, according to new data from the UNESCO Institute for Statistics. In total, more than 93 million children and youth of primary and secondary school ages are out of school across the region. At least 15 million of these children will never set foot in a classroom, with girls facing the biggest barriers.[3]

Learning to read and write is a fundamental right. Yet, 38 % of African adults (some 153 millions) are illiterate; two-thirds of these are women. Africa is the only continent where more than half of parents are not able to help their children with homework due to illiteracy.[4]

Although these statistics bring tears to the eyes, we cannot however, shy away from them. Our leaders must take responsibility for the education of all and sundry. Until we make education a priority, we would not be able to make Africa the envy of the world.

The second principle of governance that we must adopt in building Africa is racial and religious harmony. Some of the crisis that we face in Africa and that cripples economic activities and hinders our economic growth is religious crisis. Our government has to urgently foster unity between people of all religion, as this is instrumental to the development of our nation and continent.

The third principle is one that we must not take for granted at all; zero tolerance for corruption. Nothing has destroyed Africa as much as corruption has. Amidst all our wealthy natural resources, we are still the poorest continent thanks to nothing more than corruption. If we do not fight corruption in Africa, it will be impossible to develop the continent.

The fourth principle has to do with the rule of law and if you were a typical African, you would agree with me that almost every African country falls short in this regard. However, According to a World Bank study, the rule of law ranks top among the factors influencing a country's development. The ball is in our court. It is up to us now to amend our ways and follow the rule of law to the letter.

The fifth principle of governance is inclusiveness and this has to do with social equity. If each African country can treat its citizens as equal without marginalization of any particular people group, it will aid faster and wide spread development. If our government can subsidize education, housing, healthcare and public transportation for all its citizens, then we are already on our way to building a continent that the black man can call home.

The sixth and final principle of good governance is care for the environment. Africa is the dirtiest continent in the world, full of slums and untidy streets. Our sewage system is broken. Poor drainage systems and polluted water bodies are almost everywhere in our continent. If we could learn from Singapore and take good care of our environment, we would be able to replicate the kind of beautiful, clean and healthy environment in Singapore in our own country.

So, we see that great countries are great thanks to good governance. It does not matter how small and how deprived a country is in terms of natural resources, if that country can practice the principles of good governance, it would definitely become a first world country.

Unfortunately, our African leaders have failed to learn the principles of good governance. Almost all our leaders have refused to emulate and replicate the principles of governance with which nations like Singapore became great.

Fortunately for the nation of Rwanda, their president, Paul Kagame has decided to be an exception to the rest of the African leaders. He has adopted the principles of governance of Singapore and has implemented same in his country.

Many of the achievements of Kagame and his governing Rwandan Patriotic Front party are impressive. He took over a deeply divided nation in desperate need of economic and political reconstruction. Since then, Kagame has established firm personal control over Rwandan politics, generating the political stability needed for economic renewal.

Rwanda is often touted as an example of what African states could achieve if only they were better governed. Out of the ashes of a horrific genocide, President Paul Kagame has resuscitated the economy, curtailed corruption and maintained political stability all thanks to the principles of good governance.[5]

If the African continent is going to be a home to the black man, then all other countries must learn good governance from Rwanda. With good governance, all African countries can become great. Without it, no development can be achieved.

The Men Who Built America

Having discussed the importance of good governance in nation building, I would in this session love to state that the development of a nation is not the sole responsibility of the government but a shared responsibility between the government and the governed. Every citizen has a role to play in the development of a nation. It has become our habit to blame the government for everything that is lacking in our countries as if we do not have a role to play in nation building.

One of the secret of great nations is the ability of their citizens to participate in nation building. You and I can take personal responsibility for the development of our nation. America as a great nation was built by its citizens and not just the government. Americans have been taught to think about what they would do for their country instead of what their country would do for them. This has become a national value; that every citizen knows that they have a role to play in nation building.

America was built by men like Rockefeller, JP Morgan, Henry Ford, Andrew Carnegie and Cornelius. These men despite not being political leaders, worked hard to build America. They did not blame the government for lack of development, neither did they migrate to better developed countries. No! They played their role in nation building.

John D. Rockefeller took responsibility for the oil sector and brought development to it and through it made America the greatest nation on earth.

JP Morgan took responsibility for the banking industry and financed the American economy. It was thanks to him that America became one of the richest countries on earth.

Henry Ford took responsibility for the automobile industry and made it possible for most Americans to have their own cars at cheaper and affordable prices. His automobile industry contributed hugely to the American economy.

Andrew Carnegie was another great American who expanded the American steel industry and worked hard for the development of the American nation.

Cornelius Vanderbilt took over the railway system of America and contributed to the building of the American economy.

What should you learn from these men? It is the idea that nation building is not only the responsibility of government but also of the citizens. You and I must work hard to build our nations. We could dedicate our lives to the building of any sector of the economy that we feel needs to be built. We do not always have to blame the government for everything or run away to other countries to stay. Instead of running abroad and shying away from the responsibility of nation building, let us build our own nations. We can all work for the building of our nation. It was the citizens of America that built America, the citizens of Africa must also be ready to work hard to build their continent and nations.

It Is Our Continent Not Theirs!

In the final session of this chapter, I would like to draw your attention to one truth that I think we as black people often forget. That truth is that, Africa is our continent. It belongs to us not the white man. Africa does not belong to America, Europe, Asia or any other continent. Africa is the home of the black man. The continent is ours not theirs.

Why am I reminding you of what I think we should all know? It is because, whenever I listen to most Africans talk about Africa, I hear them almost always complaining and blaming the white man for the current sorry state of Africa. When an African country is facing economic crisis, the citizens begin to blame Europe or America for it. When poverty ravages an African country, everyone begins to look up to Europe and America for aid and gets angry when the aids are not forthcoming. When a country like Nigeria is in debt and cannot pay, everyone begins to look up to china for loans and get upset when china refuses. When a country like Democratic republic of Congo is unable to achieve developmental growth, they put the blame on their colonial masters who left their land and granted them independence many decades ago. There is almost no African country who does not blame colonial masters as the reason they are not able to develop and become a first world country.

The truth is that, we often forget that the African continent is ours and that it is our responsibility to develop and build it. America does not owe us any aid. Europe does not owe us any help. China is not under any obligation to give us financial loan. The African continent is ours and not theirs. If we are going to build an African continent that we can call home, you and I must stop depending on foreign nations and erase that entitlement mentality from our minds. It is an act of abdicating our responsibility to the white man if we depend on them to build our continent for us and blame them for the backwardness and lack of progress in Africa.

We should rather hold our own leaders accountable for the pitiable state of Africa. Our leaders must be held accountable for the corruption and bribery that has crippled our economy. Our leaders must be made to answer for their inability to develop the African continent.

In reporting a speech by President Barack Obama in 2009, Alex Spillius wrote an article on the Telegraph titled *"Barack Obama tells Africa to stop blaming colonialism for problems:*

President Barack Obama has told African leaders it is time to stop blaming colonialism and "Western oppression" for the continent's manifold problems."

It read thus:

Ahead of a visit to Ghana at the weekend, he said: "Ultimately, I'm a big believer that Africans are responsible for Africa.

"I think part of what's hampered advancement in Africa is that for many years we've made excuses about corruption or poor governance, that this was somehow the consequence of neo-colonialism, or the West has been oppressive, or racism – I'm not a big – I'm not a believer in excuses.

Mr. Obama, the son of a Kenyan, added: "I'd say I'm probably as knowledgeable about African history as anybody who's occupied my office. And I can give you chapter and verse on why the colonial maps that were drawn helped to spur on conflict, and the terms of trade that were uneven emerging out of colonialism.

"And yet the fact is we're in 2009," continued the US president. "The West and the United States has not been responsible for what's happened to Zimbabwe's economy over the last 15 or 20 years.

"It hasn't been responsible for some of the disastrous policies that we've seen elsewhere in Africa. And I think that it's very important for African leadership to take responsibility and be held accountable."[6]

Dear friend, I quite agree with Barack Obama. African leadership should take responsibility and be held accountable for Africa's underdevelopment. This is 2019 for God sake! About 60years after independence and we are still blaming the colonial masters? That is the height of irresponsibility.

We have the gold, the diamonds, the oil, and every mineral resource you can think of in Africa. Why should we still depend on China for loans or on America for aid? Why should the United Kingdom take the blame for the huge number of out-of-school children in Nigeria! Why should Belgium take the blame for the economic poverty of DR. Congo! How could we have everything that should make a nation rich and yet be poor! We are a greatly endowed continent. If we cannot convert our wealth of human and natural resources into economic riches and development, we have ourselves to blame. The continent is ours! Leave the white man out of it!

In conclusion of this chapter, I want to remind you that the continent of Africa belongs to us and not to the white man; hence we must all join hands to build our continent ourselves instead of waiting on the white man to do it for us.

Nuggets 6

1. It is not enough to seek self-governance or independence; one must be ready to learn the right principles of governance as well. Otherwise, the result would be an impoverished and economically stunted nation.

2. Every African nation can become a first world nation by simply employing the right principle of government. All we need are leaders who are able to learn the right principles of government and citizens who are willing to live by them.

3. It is possible to turn poverty-stricken third world African countries into first world countries. The only thing we need is the right principles of government.

4. We need to give priority to education in Africa. One of the reasons for Africa's backwardness and stunted growth is illiteracy.

5. Amidst all our wealthy natural resources, we are still the poorest continent thanks to nothing more than corruption. If we do not fight corruption in Africa, it will be impossible to develop the continent.

6. It does not matter how small and how deprived a country is in terms of natural resources, if that country can practice the principles of good

governance, it would definitely become a first world country.

7. With good governance, all African countries can become great. Without it, no development can be achieved.

8. Nation building is not only the responsibility of government but also of the citizens. You and I must work hard to build our nations.

9. Instead of running abroad and shying away from the responsibility of nation building, let us build our own nations.

10. We are a greatly endowed continent. If we cannot convert our wealth of human and natural resources into economic riches and development, we have ourselves to blame. The continent is ours! Leave the white man out of it!

CHAPTER SEVEN

Modern Day Slavery- A Choice

I am glad to welcome you to this chapter. In the previous chapter, we discussed the need to for good governance, why every black man should take responsibility for building Africa and why the white man should not be blamed for Africa's problems.

In this chapter, however, we shall discuss why instead of blaming the white man for slavery and racism, we should rather blame ourselves for the choices we've made.

The Favor That Ends in Labor

I want to express my disgust for the kind of slavery currently going on in Africa. I would like to describe it as modern day slavery. This kind of slavery is not one that is imposed on you against your will but one that you consciously and willingly choose to submit to. It is a kind of slavery that gives you bait and allows you chose to be enslaved by it or remain free. This bait is usually in the form of a favor. However, this favor eventually ends in labor. Yes! There is a kind of favor that ends up in labor or slavery.

What am I talking about? Let me explain it to you.

I want you to imagine three different scenarios. The first scenario is one in which British military men invaded African countries, took black men, women and children hostage, exports them by force to the UK and rules over them with an iron fist. This they do by suppressing the will of the people, putting yoke on their necks, using them for dishonorable jobs and threatening them with guns.

The second scenario I want you to imagine is one in which, 21st century black men, women and children take their little belongings, set out on a journey to Libya; with the goal of reaching Europe. They are not forced with a gun nor bound in chins and dragged along to Europe. No! They submit themselves willingly, with the hope of going to the white man's land to serve him in whatever way; as long as that will bring money.

The third scenario I want you to imagine is one in which an African country takes loans worth $328 million from China for infrastructural development. In this contract, the Chinese insist that only Chinese companies and contractors will be allowed to execute these projects in Africa. Then imagine that the African country is not able to pay back the loan to China and becomes perpetually indebted to china.

Fighting the Lifesaver

Having said in the previous session that we all need to fight for the freedom of the black man and the African continent, I must say here that it is however, a tragedy that Africa as it is today is in the habit of fighting those who have been sent to rescue and save her from oppression and slavery. All through history, whenever a people are to be set free from oppression, marginalization and slavery, God sends a deliverer to liberate them. It behooves on the oppressed to accept their deliverer and allow him achieve their deliverance. Nonetheless, not all oppressed people desire freedom. Some are in love with their oppressors and fights against whoever seeks to canvass for their freedom. Others are completely ignorant of their enslaved states.

It was **Harriet Tubman** who was credited with the saying:

I freed 1000 slaves. I could have freed 1000 more if only they knew they were slaves.

According to Jewish history, when God wanted to set the Jews free from their captivity to the Egyptian tyrant; Pharaoh, He sent a deliverer by the name of Moses. The same was the case with peter; when he was in Prison, God sent an angel to bring him out. God is always interested in sending a lifesaver, a deliverer or a savior to rescue an enslaved people. That is why all through history, we see different people who at different times come to the frontline to fight for the freedom of a given people or nation. Africa is not an exception.

Having said that, I would like to state here that a deliverer, savior or lifesaver can only deliver or save a willing people. If a people are not willing to be set free, there is no amount of help offered to rescue them, can save them from their chains. That is why Africans can never be set free from political slavery until the people themselves are willing to be set free. As long as the people love their oppressors, they would remain in oppression. Not even God would be able to help a people who are not willing to be helped.

In the scriptures, we see Jesus speaking concerning Jerusalem:

34 "O Jerusalem, Jerusalem! The city that murders the prophets. The city that stones those sent to help her. How often I have wanted to gather your children together even as a hen protects her brood under her wings, but you wouldn't let me. 35 And now—now your house is left desolate. And you will never again see me until you say, 'Welcome to him who comes in the name of the Lord.'"

(Luke 13:34-35 TLB)

From the passage above, we see how the Jews repeatedly killed the prophets that were sent to help them. Jesus lamented the blatant refusal of the Jewish people to allow him save them. He said" How often I have wanted to gather and protect your children, but you wouldn't let me" What followed was a heartbreaking statement" Now your house is left desolate"

What do we see from these statements? We see the result of refusing to accept help or resisting your deliverer. Just the way, Jerusalem was left desolate for fighting against her savior and deliverer, so shall Africa be left desolate if Africans themselves keep fighting against those who have been sent to help them and birth their total deliverance from political slavery and tyranny. In fact, it is an obvious fact that one of the reasons Africa is as backward and underdeveloped as it is today, is that the black man keeps fighting against his deliverer and loving his oppressors.

A typical example to buttress the point I am trying to make here is the just concluded presidential elections in Nigeria. Nigeria has two prominent political parties APC and PDP comprising of politicians who for the past few decades have oppressed the Nigerian people, stolen the commonwealth of the nation to themselves and brought untold hardship and economic woes on the people. However, when one would have thought that the Nigerian people would revolt against their oppressors and vote them out of office, the reverse was the case. The Nigerian people, a large majority of them voted in support of their oppressors (APC and PDP) and mocked, neglected, voted against and resisted the new political parties made up of younger, vision-driven and better-enlightened candidates; those whom in my opinion and I believe in the opinion of many well-meaning Nigerians, are the deliverers or saviors sent to rescue Nigerians from political tyranny and underdevelopment. The scenario is the same for many other African countries. The people keep voting in their oppressors and kicking against their saviors.

The result of such attitude is a continent that is enslaved, not by the colonial masters but by its own political tyrants. These political tyrants hold on to power for as long as they wish and the people who are under their slavery have no will power to fight for their freedom. They are complacent with slavery.

It is true that most African leaders love to cling to power. And this is not because they have the know-how to develop their country and build a continent that the black man can call home, but rather because of their greed and selfish ambitions.

Any African ruler who has tarried in office for over two decades, yet the bulk of his people still live below the poverty line, deserves to step aside regardless of his continuous fictional plans on paper, and allow someone else take up the opportunity of either succeeding or failing on the job!

Unfortunately, the political tyrants would not give up their powerful seats until the people awaken to fight for their rights.

Below are some of the rulers and political masters that held Africa hostage in underdevelopment and economic woes.

Robert Mugabe: 93years old Zimbabwean President. Was in power since Zimbabwe's independence (almost four decades) and intended to re-contest in 2018 but was ousted from office.

I would like us to analyze these three scenarios and what they mean.

In the first instance, what we see is a typical example of the transatlantic slave trade that took place for about 400years in which black men and women were forcefully sold into slavery against their will. For such kind of slavery, the whole world condemned the act and worked hard to abolish it. For such kind of slavery I have already advocated forgiveness and reconciliation between the black race and the white race.

In the second instance, we see black men and women whose fore fathers fought so hard to be liberated from colonialism and slavery to the white man, to achieve independence, enslaving themselves again willingly to the white man all in a search for greener pastures. These ones are ready to become subservient to the white man not against their will but willingly. They get a favor of travelling abroad only to get there and become slaves again to the white man. This is modern day slavery.

In the third instance, we see an African country possibly becoming financially indebted to China. This also is a form of modern day slavery in which an entire nation is enslaved to a superior nation. It is a favor that leads to slavery. This is exactly what the writer of proverbs meant when he said:

The rich rule over the poor, and the borrower is slave to the lender.

(Proverbs 22:7 NIV)

So, what is my point in all these? The point I want to make is that today, the white man no longer forcefully enslaves us. We make a choice to become his slaves. We therefore, do not need to blame the white man but ourselves and our leaders who have failed to despite the huge resources available to us in Africa, develop this continent. If people are risking their lives crossing the Mediterranean just to reach Europe to become slaves to the white man, it is because the black man has refused to build his home-Africa. Until we make it a point of duty to develop Africa to a point in which we would no longer need to borrow money from China or travel abroad looking for greener pastures, we would continually remain victims of modern-day slavery. It is unfortunate that our leaders are not yet ready to build an African continent that every black person can call home. Rather, they turn the continent into a jungle of oppression; to oppress their fellow black men.

The Jungle of Oppression

During the Soviet dictatorship of Stalin, Stalin came to one meeting of his top generals with a live chicken. He started to pluck its feathers one by one off.[1]

The chicken quacked in pain, blood oozing from its pores. It gave out heartbreaking cries but Stalin continued without remorse plucking feather after feather until the chicken was completely naked.

After that, he threw the chicken on the ground and from his pockets, took out some chicken feed and started to throw it at the poor creature.

It started eating and as he walked away, the chicken followed him and sat at his feet feeding from his hand.

Stalin then told members of his party leadership

"This chicken represents the people; you must disempower them, brutalize them, beat them up and leave them. If you do this and then give them peanuts when they are in that helpless and desperate situation, they will blindly follow you for the rest of their life.

They will think you are a hero forever. They will forget that, it is you who brought them to that situation in the first place."

This is the way of the oppressor, a method well known to the Nigerian elites, especially the politicians.[2]

There is no better word to describe Africa today than it being called a jungle of oppression. The kind of oppression going on in Africa today is heartbreaking. It is not the white man oppressing the black man as in the days of Nelson Mandela and Martin Luther King Jnr. It is the black man oppressing his fellow black man. It is the rich black man oppressing the poor black man. It is the powerful black politician oppressing his black subjects. Africa right from her post-independence years has produced not a few tyrants' leaders who oppress and kill their own citizens;

More than 600,000 Lango and Acholi tribesmen perished at the hands of Idi Amin, and co. When Idi Amin was killing off Ugandans at the rate of 100 a day, the world and even the Organization of African Unity (OAU) did nothing.

One Ugandan Anglican bishop, Festo Kivengere, was quite irate: "The OAU's silence encouraged and indirectly contributed to the bloodshed in Africa. I mean, the OAU even went so far as to go to Kampala [Uganda] for its 1975 summit and make Amin its chairman. And at the very moment the heads of state were meeting in the conference hall, talking about the lack of human rights in southern Africa, three blocks away in Amin's torture chambers, my countrymen's heads were being smashed ...."

History records that in Angola, Burundi, Chad, Ethiopia, Mozambique, Somalia, Sudan, Uganda, and other African countries, tyranny reigned. Political oppression, civil war, ruinous strife, and chaos ravage black Africa. More than 8 million African peasants have fled their villages to escape the generalized state of violence and terror.[3]

Fast forward to 2019, across sub-Saharan Africa, many groups are excluded from political participation because of their ethnicity, religion, gender or region. They often face violence, threats, neglect, and exploitation. The political oppression of these groups is systematic and primarily state-driven.[4]

It is impossible to call Africa home when you are oppressed and deprived in your own country and continent. Little wonder our people run abroad to Europe and America where in most cases they are treated with more dignity and respect by the white man than they are treated at home by their tyrant leaders. It is impossible to build a nation like this. Where there is oppression, a continent can only regress and go backward in development.

If we are going to build a civilized Africa, the various kinds of oppression that is prevalent in Africa must be stopped. Only then can we create an Africa that we all would be proud of.

Blame Slavery Not Racism

All over Africa, I see my fellow black man accusing the white man of racism and blaming racism as one of the factors responsible for Africa's underdevelopment. To that, I strongly disagree. I do not think that racism has anything to do with our backwardness in Africa. I have stated in this book several factors that are responsible for the pitiable state of Africa and I do not consider racism as one of them. It is all a mindset thing. It is in our mind that we assume that our problems in Africa are born out of racism. If we should ever blame anything for our underdevelopment it should be slavery and not racism. By slavery, I do not mean the act of slavery itself, but the mindset that it created in the black man. That mindset that makes us feel that we are inferior, incapacitated and unable to build our nation ourselves.

We should rather blame slavery for the backwardness in Africa and not racism. Africa's problem has nothing to do with racism but so much to do with slavery and the mentality it bred.

We should blame the slavery that our leaders have imposed on us via oppression and tyranny. We should blame the slavery that we consciously submit to by leaving our lands desolate and running to the white man's land to serve him in forced labor. We should blame the slavery that our leaders cause by taking loans from other countries which they cannot pay back.

Forget about racism. It is not our problem. Our problem is our corrupt leaders. Our problem is our wrong mindset. Our problem is our low self-esteem. Our problem is not racism, it is ignorance. Our problem is not racism; it is our failure to harness our natural resources. Our problem is not racism; it is our failure to plan. Our problem is not racism; it is our love for status quo. Stop blaming the white man for Africa's economic woes; blame the black citizens of Africa who have refused to elect visionary leaders. Racism is not our problem! We are our own problems.

Nuggets 7

1. Until we make it a point of duty to develop Africa to a point in which we would no longer need to borrow money from China or travel abroad looking for greener pastures, we would continually remain victims of modern-day slavery.

2. If people are risking their lives crossing the Mediterranean just to reach Europe to become slaves to the white man, it is because the black man has refused to build his home-Africa.

3. Forget about racism. It is not our problem. Our problem is our corrupt leaders. Our problem is our wrong mindset. Our problem is our low self-esteem.

4. Our problem is not racism, it is ignorance. Our problem is not racism; it is our failure to harness our natural resources. Our problem is not racism; it is our failure to plan

5. Stop blaming the white man for Africa's economic woes; blame the black citizens of Africa who have refused to elect visionary leaders.

CHAPTER EIGHT

The Road to Exile

In the previous chapter we discussed the concept of modern day slavery and how African leaders oppress their subordinates. In this chapter, we shall in details discuss how African people as a result of the harsh living conditions on the continent set themselves on a journey to exile.

The Quest for a Safe-Haven

According to the Cambridge dictionary, a safe haven is a place where you are protected from harm or danger. It is a known fact that Africa is no longer safe for its inhabitants. The increase in disease rate, death rate, maternal mortality, road traffic accidents, political unrest, ethnic crisis, terrorism, hunger, unemployment and starvation etc., has made Africa unsafe for its citizens. Africa therefore, cannot be said to be a safe haven.

If the citizens of Africa are not safe in their own continent and cannot call Africa home, they are left with no option than to seek safety elsewhere. The black man is left without a place in his continent he can call home. This is a tragic situation and a shameful one also. Our leaders should be ashamed and weep that after close to sixty years post-independence, they cannot build a safe haven for their people.

In a national economic meeting with Nigerian Vice President Yemi Osibanjo last year, the chairman of Bill and Melinda Gates foundation, Bill Gates said:

"Nigeria is one of the most dangerous places in the world to give birth with the fourth worst maternal mortality rate in the world ahead of only Sierra Leone, Central African Republic and Chad. One in three Nigerian children is chronically malnourished.[1]

Bill Gates was right; Nigeria is one of the most dangerous places to give birth. More than that, life generally in Africa is hard and unfriendly. Our health care is not functional. Our electricity is not functional, our universities are not functional. Almost everything is abnormal in Africa. So, one must understand why Africans run out of Africa in search of a safe haven. And mind you, this has nothing to do with the white man as I have stated earlier. It is entirely our fault.

In trying to run away from the dangerous and harsh conditions in Africa, most Africans run into bigger problems and eventually lost their lives.

Lost In the Ocean

The story of how Africans troop in their numbers from the African soil to go seek a safe haven in European and American countries is a sad one. The ordeal that Africans go through trying to cross the oceans and the deserts to arrive Europe, an exile journey that claims the lives of many is one that breaks my heart.

More than 200 migrants drowned at sea in the Mediterranean in three days, making the death toll in a year equal to more than 1,000.

The 1,000 deaths landmark was reached on 1 July 2018. It is the fourth year in succession that more than 1,000 migrants have died trying to reach Europe via the Mediterranean Sea.[2]

They know their lives are at risk, yet each year thousands of people from Africa, the Middle East and beyond – civil war refugees, political asylum seekers and economic migrants – leave their homelands and try to reach the 'promised' land of Europe.

In fact, the last decade alone has seen an upsurge in the number of Africans taking to the sea in search of safety, economic opportunities, or both in places such as Italy, France, Germany and the United Kingdom. These migrants believe that European countries and others like them represent an opportunity for them to pursue safety and economic stability.

However, danger often awaits those who include a sea route in their flight from developing countries such as Eritrea, Libya, Morocco, and several West African countries. It is believed that most people who die at sea are those fleeing either political or economic instabilities in their countries of origin, in anticipation of a better life. But how do they get there?

Their journey is atrocious to say the least. Indeed, recent research carried out by the International Organization for Migration (IOM) confirms that after getting paid huge sums of money by would-be migrants, people-smugglers crowd migrants into decrepit ships, often placed in perilous situations with no safety precautions, no drinking water and no food for the entire journey.

In many cases, these unscrupulous organised gangs ship up to 1000 people freely simply because there is no organisation at the global level currently responsible for systematically monitoring these crossing routes.

Recent headlines are full of tragedies, and many more go undetected. The scale of the problem is hard to measure, as many ships and bodies disappear into the sea. However, in September 2014, a report by IOM stated that migrants trying to reach more prosperous countries in Europe have died at a rate of eight every day for the past 14 years.

The report indicates that since research was undertaken in 2000, almost 40,000 people have died on worldwide migrant routes, with 22,000 of them trying to cross over from Africa to Europe. And, although Eritreans and

Somalis make up the biggest groups, they are increasingly joined by swelling crowds of Syrians fleeing their civil war-racked country escaping lawlessness and sectarian strife, and by political refugees from Libya, Central African Republic, South Sudan, Chad, Nigeria, to name but a few. It is important to note that since many ships sink at sea, the true number of fatalities is likely to be even higher than the figures reported by IOM.[3]

What a waste of precious lives! All because we have refused to build and develop our land. What a waste of precious lives! All because our leaders have failed to, empower their citizens. We have all the mineral resources in our land, yet we cannot build a home for our citizens. We leave them to die and get lost in the sea in search of a safe haven. Oh! Africa. Who has bewitched us?

Who Wants To Return From Exile!

According to Collins English dictionary, if someone is living in exile, they are living in a foreign country because they cannot live in their own country, usually for political reasons.

Today, there are millions of black people of African origin leaving outside the continent of Africa. They have refused to return to their countries back in Africa not because they were sent on exile for political reasons but because they feel more at home abroad than in Africa. This is a kind of self-imposed exile. Most of these people have become citizens of the countries in which they reside and have completely forgotten that they are from Africa; the home of the black race.

There are black people in Europe and America who are medical professionals, business consultants, lawyers, engineers etc. and who are using their expertise and professional knowledge to contribute positively to the economic growth of other nations while Africa is in economic poverty and recession.

One of the best neurosurgeons in the world Dr. Ben Carson is a black man residing in the USA and currently the United States Secretary of Housing and Urban Development.

In 1997, Carson and his team went to Zambia in South Central Africa to separate infant boys Luka and Joseph Banda. This operation was especially difficult because the boys were joined at the tops of their heads, facing in opposite directions, making it the first time a surgery of this type had been performed. After a 28-hour operation that was supported by previously rendered 3-D mapping both boys survived and neither suffered brain damage.[4]

Another black man who is doing exploits in a foreign land is Dr. Chris Imafidon, who is from Edo State, Nigeria. He is an ophthalmologist based in London. He is a renowned scholar who has taught at Oxford, Harvard and Cambridge Universities at various times and consults for the United Kingdom, United States and other governments. He recently presented new evidence to support his theory that there is a genius in every child, and asks society to do all it can to develop each child's talent even if the child is from the poorest background.

Chris is a multi-award winning researcher, and member of the Information Age Executive Round-table forum - which is made up of the top 15 IT experts, decision-makers, CIOs, and executives in the UK. He is a consultant to governments and industry leaders.[5]

Have you heard of Dr. Oluyinka Olutoye?

NIGERIA shone brightly on the global stage as the news broke just recently of a successful surgery a team of medical doctors, led by Nigerian-born Dr. Oluyinka Olutoye, carried on an unborn baby at a Texas hospital in the US.

According to medical reports, the unborn baby had sacrococcygeal teratoma, a rare tumor that appeared at the base of the baby's tailbone. These types of tumors, it is estimated, occur in about one of 40,000 pregnancies, and if left unchecked, could continue taking the baby's blood supply and eventually cause heart failure.

Oluyinka Olutoye and Darrell Cass, alongside a team of about 20 others, performed an unbelievable 'miracle' when it carried out a successful surgery on the unborn baby to remove the tumor and returned it to the mother's womb; a feat that has generated global recognition of the baby as the baby born twice.

To carry out the operation on the baby named Lynlee Hope at 23 weeks, Olutoye and his team removed her from her mother's womb, operated on her and then returned her to the womb where the injuries from her operation healed and she continued to grow until she was born again at 36 weeks.[6]

We all know the name Barack Obama, the 44th President of the United States and the first African-American U.S. President.

Obama, who is of Kenyan origin, was elected to the Presidency of America in 2008, and won the re-election in 2012.[7]

As the first African-American elected President of the United States, Barack Obama became a pivotal figure in American history even before his inauguration. But after winning a second term in 2012, his achievements in office have made him one of the most transformative presidents of the past hundred years. He took office with a country in peril and led it through the Great Recession, two wars, civil unrest, a rash of mass shootings, and changing cultural demographics. In the 2008 campaign he called for change and eight years later we are living in a more prosperous country because of it. As president of America, He rescued the country from the Great Recession, cutting the unemployment rate from 10% to 4.7% over six years amongst numerous other achievements that I will not mention here for want of space.[7]

Barack Obama was able to prove that an African-American could become America's first black president and lead his country to prosperity.

In this session, I have written about Ben Carson, Chris Imafidon, Olutoye Oluyinka and Barack Obama. However, these are less than 1% of the black African sons and daughters who are doing exploits all over the globe; from Europe to America, from Australia to Asia and in every nook and cranny of the world. Africans all over the world have been able to display intelligence, expertise, creative ability and leadership prowess anywhere they find themselves.

However, it is unbelievable that most of our black people who are educated in the west and civilized nations of the world don't want to return home and share their skills to develop the African continent. They have become like politicians sent on exile and who are banned from returning home. This is rather an unfortunate situation and needs to be corrected.

Can you imagine how Africa would be like if all black professionals in every field who are abroad take it as a responsibility to develop Africa with their expertise! Can you imagine if the IT (information technology) specialists saturate Africa with IT training centers or the leadership experts setting up leadership training schools in every nook and cranny of the African continent! What about our neurosurgeons and medical professionals abroad coming home to share their knowledge with Africans!

Wouldn't Africa become as developed as the rest of the world?

It is my belief that if all black sons and daughters abroad contribute in building the African continent, Africa would become a place that we all can call home in no distant time.

Let's stop calling on the white man to build Africa or blaming them for the lack of development in our land. We Africans can develop our land by ourselves. We only need to return from exile and join forces with the rest of us back home to build our land. If Africa must change for the better, we must stop waiting for the white man and start taking responsibility by ourselves. And in the words of Barack Obama, I want to say:

"Change will not come if we wait for some other person or some other time. We are the ones we've been waiting for. We are the change that we seek."

-Barack Obama

Nuggets 8

1. Our leaders should be ashamed and weep that after close to sixty years post-independence, they cannot build a safe haven for their people.
2. It is my belief that if all black sons and daughters abroad contribute in building the African

continent, Africa would become a place that we all can call home in no distant time.

3. Let's stop calling on the white man to build Africa or blaming them for the lack of development in our land. We Africans can develop our land by ourselves. We only need to return from exile and join forces with the rest of us back home to build our land.

4. If Africa must change for the better, we must stop waiting for the white man and start taking responsibility by ourselves.

CHAPTER NINE

Could Religion Be The Answer!

I am glad to welcome you to the penultimate chapter of this book. In the previous chapter we discussed the need for Africans all over the globe to return from their self-imposed exile and come contribute to building Africa.

In this chapter, we shall discuss the role religion has played in contributing to the state of things in Africa and why we urgently need a reformation.

Religion and Its Effect on Civilization

One question I would like to answer in this session is whether religion has any role to play in the development of nations.

We already know that Africa is the least developed and poorest continent in the world. Almost everywhere you turn in Africa, you would see failure in education, in electricity supply, in politics, in security, and so on.

The government has failed the people and the only hope for the masses is turning to God for solution.

All over Africa, people are found praying earnestly and begging God to come develop our continent for us. They think that the solution to Africa's underdevelopment is in the hand of God and thus are calling on Him every day to show up and do his job. Unfortunately, most Africans are not aware that the responsibility for nation building lies with man and not God. God does not build hospitals, housing, stadiums or roads. It is not God who built the state-of-the-art hospitals in Europe and America. God was not among the engineers who built the sky scrapers in Singapore and Dubai. No! God does not develop nations, men do.

God has given us everything we need to develop Africa. He has blessed us with all kinds of mineral resources that could make our continent the richest and most developed continent on the globe. But to come down and develop Africa for us, No! He will not.

We can pray all we want and fast as much as we can, God will not come down to develop Africa. Prayers do not develop nations, creative thinking, hard work and building infrastructures do. We cannot just fold our arms and pray to God and expect economic growth.

All growth depends upon activity. There is no development physically or intellectually without effort, and effort means work."

– Calvin Coolidge

God has given us brains and intellectual capacity so that we can create the kind of continent we want. To keep calling on God to develop Africa for us is an act of trying to abdicate our responsibility to God. That shows that we are irresponsible people.

Africa is a deeply religious continent and has some of the largest church cathedrals in the world. Every single day, most Africans go to church from bible studies, to prayer meetings, to choir rehearsals and revival meetings. How does this affect our economic growth and development?

There is a direct relationship between religion and laziness, leading to poverty in our part of the world. A lot of believers would rather spend their time attending one religious event or the other throughout the year at the expense of their work or source of livelihood. It is not uncommon to see church services from morning till evening in any part of the country, even on weekdays. There is no doubt that the more time a person spends at his/her religious program to the neglect of his/her work, the less income the person earns, leading to lack and poverty.[1]

I think our problem is that we do not stop to question our actions. The question we fail to ask ourselves is "what is the effect of our religiosity on the development of our continent?" How could we be the most religious continent in the world and yet the poorest and least developed!

A careful study of most of the highly developed nations in the world would reveal to you that they are not as religious as Africa. Yet they are developed and have everything we are praying for in Africa.

A highly developed country like Norway has only 2% of the population attending church on weekly basis. Russia has 2% church attendance, Japan, 3% church attendance, and China, 9% church attendance. However, a 2013 report says that Nigeria, an African country has as much as 89% church attendance rate. It is obvious why Africa is a backward continent. There is no way we would become a leading continent when we spend all our time in church praying while other nations invest their time in the laboratory, library, at the workshop, in computer training classes etc. We cannot pray away underdevelopment, we can only work hard and learn how other nations were able to develop. Upon gaining that knowledge, we must go ahead and implement what we have learnt to develop our land.

For Africa, religion has not aided our civilization. It has rather slowed it. Religion has played a huge role in the backwardness and lack of development in Africa.

In Northern Nigeria for example, there is the terrorist group called Boko Haram. What does that name mean? It means Western education is forbidden. The group is in strong opposition to Western education, and wants to impose Islamic religious law as the only law in Nigeria. As a result, they have killed people in their thousands, burnt houses and industrial complexes, driven out foreign investors and hampered economic activities.

I believe you will agree with me that religion has done so much harm to the civilization and development of Africa. Until we downplay religion in Africa, we would hardly be able to develop the continent to compete with the rest of the world.

Pastors and Politicians

There are two groups of people that have contributed immensely to the retarded growth of the Nigerian economy. They are pastors and politicians. It is unfortunate that the two set of people who should lead the citizens of every nation to economic prosperity have rather destroyed the nation's economy.

While politicians embezzle government funds, pastors defraud people with all kinds of false gospels that are centered on money and materialism. He said most of these pastors and politicians waste their stolen money on a lavished lifestyle at the detriment of the poor masses.

Although Africa is home to some of the poorest and most religious countries in the world, it may seem a bit contradictory to note that she is home to the richest pastors in the world. According to naija.com, a Nigerian blog, five African pastors were listed among the wealthiest men of God in the world. They include Bishop Oyedepo with a net worth of $150 million, Chris Oyakilome with a net worth of $50 million, T.B Joshua with $15 million while Chris Okotie and Matthew Asimilowo stands at $10 each.

It is commonplace in Africa for pastors to own mega churches, fleet of cars, private jets and properties all over the world while a majority of their members can barely feed on a daily basis.[2]

It is a hard thing to imagine that African pastors are building empires and living lavished lifestyles while Africans groan in poverty. That is the height of wickedness; to fleece the flock of God instead of feed them.

For politicians, the amount of money they steal yearly from Africa is alarming.

Globally, extreme poverty has been halved in 20 years, and could be virtually wiped out by 2030. But much of the progress that has been made is at risk - not because of natural disasters or new diseases, but because of something far more insidious.

Analysis by The ONE Campaign suggests that at least $1 trillion is being taken out of developing countries each year through a web of corrupt activity that involves shady deals for natural resources, the use of anonymous shell companies, money laundering and illegal tax evasion. Massive sums are being taken out of developing countries' own budgets and economies, preventing them from financing their own fight against extreme poverty, disease and hunger. It is nothing short of a trillion-dollar scandal.[3]

If the money was retained by the developing nations, it could help avert 3.6m deaths a year between 2015 and

2025. It would also mean that these countries would no longer need to rely on overseas aid from rich nations.

The report found that $3.2trn of the world's undeclared assets originated in developing countries like those in Africa. If the missing millions were taxed, it could bring revenue of $19.5bn a year.

In Sub Saharan African alone, curbing corruption could educate extra 10m children a year; provide antiretroviral drugs for more than 1m people with HIV/AIDS and pay more almost 16.5m vaccines.[4]

From the foregoing, you will agree with me that the white man is not our enemy, we are our own enemies. Our politicians are the real enemies of progress in Africa.

David Cameroon was alleged to have said *"If the amount of money stolen from Nigeria in the last 30 years was stolen from the UK, the UK would cease to exist,"*

Who is stealing Africa's money, the white man? No, African Politicians! Who is impoverishing the citizens of Africa, Europe and America? No, African politicians and pastors!

Don't tell me about racism, it is not our problem. Don't tell me about the slave trade, it is not our problem. Don't complain about colonialism, it is not even the least of our problems. Our greatest problem is corruption; not by the white man but by our fellow black men. Until we kill corruption, Africa can never become a developed continent. Until our pastors and politicians stop embezzling the common wealth of the masses, we would keep praying to God to come down and develop Africa and nothing will happen.

The Need for Reformation (The Protestant Reformation)

As a student of history, I read about the protestant reformation and how it transformed the whole of Europe.

According to Mr. Weber the Industrial Revolution that gave birth to the new economy in Europe and eventually to our modern civilization, was a result of the teachings of the European Protestants.

Max Weber, the author of the book "The Protestant Ethic and the Spirit of Capitalism." Explained the role the Protestants played in forming the new economy of the old world.

Weber believed that when the Protestant ethic influenced large numbers of people to engage in work in the secular world, in enterprises, in trade, in savings, in investments, these gave birth to the new world economy, that is largely known as capitalism. It is upon that economy that our modern world stands.

Social scientists don't doubt the fact that the European civilization which is the civilization the whole world enjoys today, was as a result of the direct teachings of the early Protestants.

If the teachings of the early Christians changed Rome and the entire Roman Empire, we can't point to any great change that the teachings coming from our pulpits today are producing upon our world in general. If the teachings of the Protestants in Europe gave birth to the Protestant ethics and the modern civilization, it becomes alarming that most of our charismatic teachings today mainly concentrate on individual aggrandizement.[5]

When this kind of religion practiced in Nigeria and Africa is juxtaposed with the protestant reformation that transformed most of Europe, it becomes obvious that our religion must be a different kind of religion and a far cry from that which built Europe.

To build Africa, we must have a reformation; the kind of reformation that developed Europe. We must begin to teach our people that it is better to work than to pray and wait on God for national development. Our pastors must stop telling people to come to church every day and encourage them to go to the libraries and laboratories to do research.

Africa needs real reformation both in our churches and in our political leadership, as this is the only way Africa can become a continent that is enviable by all and sundry.

Nuggets 9

1. It is not God who built the state-of-the-art hospitals in Europe and America. God was not among the engineers who built the sky scrapers in Singapore and Dubai. No! God does not develop nations, men do.

2. God has given us everything we need to develop Africa. He has blessed us with all kinds of mineral resources that could make our continent the richest and most developed continent on the globe. But to come down and develop Africa for us, No! He will not.

3. We can pray all we want and fast as much as we can, God will not come down to develop Africa. Prayers do not develop nations, creative thinking, hard work and building infrastructures do. We cannot just fold our arms and pray to God and expect economic growth.

4. God has given us brains and intellectual capacity so that we can create the kind of continent we want. To keep calling on God to develop Africa for us is an act of trying to abdicate our responsibility to God. That shows that we are irresponsible people.

5. For Africa, religion has not aided our civilization. It has rather slowed it. Religion has played a huge role in the backwardness and lack of development in Africa.

6. Don't tell me about racism, it is not our problem. Don't tell me about the slave trade, it is not our

problem. Don't complain about colonialism, it is not even the least of our problems. Our greatest problem is corruption; not by the white man but by our fellow black men.

7. Until we kill corruption, Africa can never become a developed continent. Until our pastors and politicians stop embezzling the common wealth of the masses, we would keep praying to God to come down and develop Africa and nothing will happen.

CHAPTER TEN

Arise Africa, the Future is here!

I am delighted to welcome you to the last chapter of this book. We have said so much about the sorry state of Africa, the effect of racism, colonialism and the slave trade on the development of Africa. I have also explained how our mindset as Africans has limited our progress and the need for us to renew our minds. The effect of religion and politics on the backwardness of Africa was also discussed. However, in this chapter, I am calling on Africans to arise and build their land. We must forget about the past and look to the future of Africa.

Where Are the Nehemiahs?

Every nation of the world was built by people. There is no nation in the world that was not built by somebody or a group of people.

Every house is built by someone but God is the builder of everything. Hebrews 3:4

All through history, we see that whenever nations are in crisis or in distress, God raises people to salvage the situation. He raises people from the same nation to rescue the situation. Speaking concerning Israel, God once said:

Your sons will rebuild the long-deserted ruins of your cities, and you will be known as "The People Who Rebuild Their Walls and Cities."

(Isaiah 58:12 TLB)

From the foregoing, we could see that those who would build Africa would be sons and daughters of African origin. The problems that we face in Africa today would be solved by Africans and not by Europeans or Americans. What we need in Africa now are people who would take upon themselves the responsibility of building the continent just as Nehemiah did in biblical history.

When Nehemiah heard that his people were in great trouble and disgrace and that the wall of Jerusalem was broken down, and its gates burned with fire, he sat down and wept. But more than that, Nehemiah took the responsibility of building the walls of Jerusalem upon himself and went ahead to build. Nehemiah took with him skilled men and they went to build the wall of Jerusalem. In the same vein, I am calling on every African to return home and build Africa.

No Place like Home

It is true that most Africans abroad feel at home and enjoys privileges that they would not enjoy if they return to Africa. It is true that we enjoy good health care, stable electricity, available internet, good roads and transport system, quality education and relative peace when we are abroad in the white man's land. However, I want to say that there is no place like home. No matter how comfortable we feel abroad, the truth remains that Europe, America, Australia and Asia is not our home. The best we can be abroad is second-class citizens. We would never be treated as first class citizens.

Africa is the home of the black man. Africa does not have all of the things I mentioned above, yes! But we can bring them to Africa. We can develop Africa so much so that it would compete with other continents of the world. We can make Africa our home indeed; not just a home by the things we would enjoy but also a home by origin. I want to challenge every son and daughter of Africa whether home or abroad to arise and build Africa just like Nehemiah did the walls of Jerusalem. If we do not build our home, we would keep living in the white man's land and leave our land desolate and in ruins.

It is only in Africa that we would be treated as first class citizens. If we can join hands to build this continent, we would truly enjoy and understand what it means to say "no place like home."

If you go anywhere, even paradise, you will miss your home.

--Malala Yousafzai

Africa–The Future of the World

In life seasons come and seasons go. One day it is summer and the next day it is winter. Situations do not remain the same forever.

There was a time in history when Europe ruled the world and everybody envied Europe. That was their season. When their season was over, America took over and became the leading continent and nation in the world and all of Europe and the rest of the world began to bow to and respect America. America has had her season too. Soon it would be Africa's turn to rule the world. I believe that Africa is the future of the world.

In the scripture we see that kingdoms rise and kingdoms fall. Empires rise and empires fall. Kings reign and they are eventually overtaken. That is the fact of life. The white man is ruling the world today, but tomorrow it will be the black man. Africa is the home of the black man. So, Africa is the future of the world.

The scripture explains it this way:

So the last shall be first, and the first last: for many be called, but few chosen.

Matthew 20:16

Today, Africa is last and the rest of the world first but tomorrow, Africa shall be first and the rest of the world last. However, this will not happen by miracle. It will only happen when we apply the principles that are written in this book.

To make Africa the future of the world, we must start by changing our mindsets. We must renew our minds and erase every feeling of worthlessness and inferior complex. We must know that God's creative ability is within us.

To make Africa the future of the world, every black man must learn to plan, using the power of foresight. Our leaders must sit down and plan the future of Africa.

To make Africa the future of the world, we must stop blaming racism, slave trade and colonialism for our problems but rather take responsibility for our problems and look for ways to solve them.

To make Africa the future of the world, we must stop depending on the white man for aid as though we are not an independent nation. We must rise up to the occasion and live like people who are truly free and are capable of leading Africa to greatness.

To make Africa the future of the world, we must raise young visionary leaders, retire the old men that have destroyed Africa, downgrade the status quo and enhance progressive change.

To make Africa the future of the world, we must embrace the principles of good governance, educate our people, eradicate corruption from our land, obey the rule of law, and take care of our environment.

To make Africa the future of the world, we must teach our people hard work, determination and perseverance. People must be encouraged to spend more time in the laboratories and libraries doing research than spending all week in religious gatherings.

To make Africa the future of the world, our pastors and politicians must be forced to stop embezzling the common wealth of the masses for a lavished lifestyle but rather invest into the masses and their nations at large.

To make Africa the future of the world, we must learn how to harness our huge wealth of natural resources and convert them into economic prosperity for or continent.

To make Africa the future of the world, all African sons and daughters must return home to share their expertise and professionalism with those back home so that together we can build an enviable continent.

CONCLUSION

I believe that the time has come for Africa to lead the world. And it is possible with you and me taking responsibility for our land. I know it is not going to be easy. But we shall get there if we do not faint. We shall prove to the world that our forefathers did not make a mistake by fighting for our independence. We shall show the world that we indeed have all it takes to lead a continent to prosperity. It may be difficult, but it is not impossible. And in my final words, allow me to borrow the words of Kwame Nkrumah which says:

Countrymen, the task ahead is great indeed, and heavy is the responsibility; and yet it is a noble and glorious challenge - a challenge which calls for the courage to dream, the courage to believe, the courage to dare, the courage to do, the courage to envision, the courage to fight, the courage to work, the courage to achieve - to achieve the highest excellencies and the fullest greatness of man. Dare we ask for more in life?

-Kwame Nkrumah

Africa is the home of the black man and we shall make it a home indeed; a home that the world would envy and admire. I believe it and I am committed to it. You need to believe it and be committed to it. Together, we can make Africa great again.

Nuggets 10

1. The problems that we face in Africa today would be solved by Africans and not by Europeans or Americans. What we need in Africa now are people who would take upon themselves the responsibility of building the continent just as Nehemiah did in biblical history.

2. If we do not build our home, we would keep living in the white man's land and leave our land desolate and in ruins.

3. It is only in Africa that we would be treated as first class citizens. If we can join hands to build this continent, we would truly enjoy and understand what it means to say "no place like home."

4. To make Africa the future of the world, we must embrace the principles of good governance, educate our people, eradicate corruption from our land, obey the rule of law, and take care of our environment.

5. To make Africa the future of the world, we must teach our people hard work, determination and perseverance. People must be encouraged to spend more time in the laboratories and libraries

doing research than spending all week in religious gatherings.

6. To make Africa the future of the world, our pastors and politicians must be forced to stop embezzling the common wealth of the masses for a lavished lifestyle but rather invest into the masses and their nations at large.

7. To make Africa the future of the world, we must learn how to harness our huge wealth of natural resources and convert them into economic prosperity for or continent.

8. To make Africa the future of the world, all African sons and daughters must return home to share their expertise and professionalism with those back home so that together we can build an enviable continent.

REFERENCE

Chapter One
The State of Africa in a Changing World

1. *On the poorest continent, the plight of children is dramatic, https://www.sos-usa.org/about-us/where-we-work/africa/poverty-in-africa*

2. *Black Inventors - The Complete List of Genius Black American (African American) Inventors, Scientists, and Engineers with Their Revolutionary Inventions That Changed the World and Impacted History - Part Two, https://interestingengineering.com/black-inventors-the-complete-list-of-genius-black-american-african-american-inventors-scientists-and-engineers-with-their-revolutionary-inventions-that-changed-the-world-and-impacted-history-part-two*

3. *Kwame Nkrumah: 'To-day we are here to claim this right to our independence', Motion of Destiny – 1953, https://speakola.com/political/kwame-nkrumah-motion-of-destiny-independence-1953*

Chapter Two
Rich Resources, Poor Continent

1. *8 countries with no natural resource but, thrive to become world major exporters, https://www. gamespot.com/forums/offtopic-discussion-314159273/8-countries-with-no-natural-resource-but-thrive-to-29364331/*

2. *AFRICA: A CONTINENT OF WEALTH, A CONTINENT OF POVERTY, https://waronwant.org/media/ africa-continent-wealth-continent-poverty*

Chapter Three
Rulers and the Politics of Slavery

1. *Africa's leadership failure, https://www.herald. co.zw/africas-leadership-failure/*

2. *Africa is again the world's epicenter of modern-day slavery, https://qz.com/africa/1333946/ global-slavery-index-africa-has-the-highest-rate-of-modern-day-slavery-in-the-world/*

3. *Researchers uncover Africans' part in slavery, http://edition.cnn.com/WORLD/9510/ ghana_slavery/*

4. *Political Oppression in Sub-Saharan Africa*

5. *https://www.du.edu/korbel/hrhw/researchdigest/ africa/PoliticalOppression.pdf*

6. *Africa's Injustices Aren't All to the South. Oppression by black leaders should elicit the same moral outrage heaped on South*

African apartheid, https://www.csmonitor. com/1989/0126/eayit.html

7. *Africans Crave Freedom: Yet, neither hate bondage nor love it!, http://www.therwandan. com/africans-crave-freedom-yet-neither-hate-bondage-nor-love-it/*

Chapter Four
A Historical Look at the Human Race

1. *Africa the home of human civilization, http:// www.panafricanperspective.com/origins/ earlyafricans.html*

2. *Which Continent Is The Richest In Natural Resources?, https://www.worldatlas.com/ articles/which-continent-is-the-richest-in-natural-resources.html*

3. *Arab slave trade, https://en.wikipedia.org/wiki/ Arab_slave_trade*

4. *Africa and the Transatlantic Slave Trade, http://www.bbc.co.uk/history/british/abolition/ africa_article_01.shtml*

5. *Africa-EU continental cooperation, https:// ec.europa.eu/europeaid/regions/africa/ africa-eu-continental-cooperation_en*

6. *African Americans, https://www.britannica. com/topic/African-American*

Chapter Five
How to Move Africa Forward

1. *Once Upon A Time: When 1 Dollar Was Equal To 1 Naira - Business – Nairaland, https://www.nairaland.com/2596926/once-upon-time-when-1*

2. *The 15 Oldest Presidents in Africa 2018, https://www.africanexponent.com/post/9292-africa-a-young-continent-with-old-leaders*

3. *PATRICK TRANSFORMS IRELAND, https://www.nordskogpublishing.com/patrick-transforms-ireland/*

Chapter Six
A Country and Its People

1. *The Six Principles of Good Governance, https://lkyspp.nus.edu.sg/gia/article/the-six-principles-of-good-governance*

2. *Singapore at 50: From Third World to First, https://www.thedailystar.net/op-ed/politics/singapore-50-third-world-first-123337*

3. *At least half of youth in sub-Saharan Africa are not in school, https://en.unesco.org/gem-report/sites/gem-report/files/OOSC%20SSA%20press%20release.pdf*

4. *Literacy and non-formal education, http://www.unesco.org/new/en/dakar/education/literacy/*

5. *Why Rwanda's development model wouldn't work elsewhere in Africa, http://theconversation.*

com/why-rwandas-development-model-wouldnt-work-elsewhere-in-africa-89699

6. *Barack Obama tells Africa to stop blaming colonialism for problems, https://www.telegraph.co.uk/news/worldnews/africaandindianocean/5778804/Barack-Obama-tells-Africa-to-stop-blaming-colonialism-for-problems.html*

Chapter Seven
Modern Day Slavery– A Choice

1. *You are Bigger Than Your Career—The Stalin's Chicken, https://medium.com/thrive-global/you-are-bigger-than-your-career-the-stalins-chicken-168a93f58132*

2. *THE WAY OF THE OPPRESSOR, https://www.facebook.com/olayemisuccess.fakolade/posts/2534982263210803*

3. *Africa's Injustices Aren't All to the South. Oppression by black leaders should elicit the same moral outrage heaped on South African apartheid, https://www.csmonitor.com/1989/0126/eayit.html*

4. *Political Oppression in Sub-Saharan Africa, https://www.du.edu/korbel/hrhw/researchdigest/africa/PoliticalOppression.pdf*

Chapter Eight
The Road to Exile

1. *Nigeria one of the most dangerous places to give birth – Bill Gate, https://www.vanguardngr.com/2018/03/nigeria-one-dangerous-places-give-birth-bill-gate/*

2. *Mediterranean: more than 200 migrants drown in three days, https://www.theguardian.com/world/2018/jul/03/mediterranean-migrants-drown-three-days-libya-italy*

3. *Why are so many Africans dying at sea?, https://www.newtimes.co.rw/section/read/181757*

4. *Ben Carson Biography, https://www.biography.com/people/ben-carson-475422*

5. *Dr. Chris Imafidon, https://zodml.org/discover-nigeria/people/dr-chris-imafidon#.XHrY2egzbIU*

6. *MY STORY —US-based Nigerian surgeon who operated on unborn baby, http://thenationonlineng.net/story-us-based-nigerian-surgeon-operated-unborn-baby/*

7. *Barack Obama Biography: Success Story of the 44th U.S. President, https://astrumpeople.com/barack-obama-biography/*

Chapter Nine
Could Religion Be The Answer!

1. *The Damning Effects Of Religion In Africa,*
   https://www.modernghana.com/news/712435/
   the-damning-effects-of-religion-in-africa.html

2. *African Pastors: Building Empires in the Midst*
   of Extreme Poverty, http://blog.swaliafrica.com/
   african-pastors-building-empires-in-the-midst-
   of-extreme-poverty/

3. *The Trillion Dollar Scandal, https://eurodad.*
   org/files/pdf/54115df8ef173.pdf

4. *Criminals and corrupt politicians steal $1trn*
   a year from the world's poorest countries,
   https://www.independent.co.uk/news/world/
   politics/criminals-and-corrupt-politicians-
   steal-1trn-a-year-from-the-worlds-poorest-
   countries-9707104.html

5. *The Protestant Ethic And How It Changed The*
   World, http://godembassy.com/pastor-sunday-
   adelaja/the-protestant-ethic-and-how-it-
   changed-the-world/

Printed in the United States
By Bookmasters